Jules's eyes flew wide. "What are you doing?"

If they hadn't been standing on the threshold of Franc's hotel suite in front of a hundred-ish people, the shock on her face would have made Alden laugh out loud. As it was...

"I'm touching you, my darling, and now I'm going to look at you lovingly."

Come on, Jules!

He smiled, leaning toward her so their foreheads were barely a centimeter apart. "If you could be so good as to return the favor..."

She made a sudden, small, strangled noise of acknowledgment and then her lips were curving sweetly, and her eyes were rounding into his.

"Of course, my love." Her right hand came up, covering his for a long second, and then she was drawing it down firmly, squeezing hard. "But please don't touch my hair. You paid Gerard a lot of money to make it look this good and if you mess it up, I can't fix it with just the one hand."

Merriness in her eyes, shot through with a warning.

He felt his heart wilt.

Dear Reader,

Welcome to *One Night on the French Riviera*!

This book came out of an imagined late-night phone conversation between two long-standing friends, friends who cared more for each other than they dared to admit. I imagined this a couple of years ago, wrote it down and forgot about it, until my editor suggested that I write a friends-to-lovers story.

My actor hero, Alden, was partly inspired by a boy I used to sit with on the school bus. He wanted to act and did, happily, achieve that dream, but unlike my hero, he had the support of his parents, and a lot more self-confidence. My florist heroine, Jules, arrived in my head ready-made. She is all heart. A good egg! The friend who simply cannot refuse Alden anything.

Having spent time on the French Riviera last summer, it was an obvious choice of setting. Jules and Alden retrace my own footsteps through Grasse and St. Tropez, and movie director Franc Abdali's mansion came right out of an estate agent's window in Cannes. Authentic much!

One Night on the French Riviera delivers sun and "funshine" and a whole lot of heart. I hope you enjoy it.

Ella x

One Night on the French Riviera

Ella Hayes

HARLEQUIN

Romance

Recycling programs
for this product may
not exist in your area.

ISBN-13: 978-1-335-59640-6

One Night on the French Riviera

Copyright © 2023 by Ella Hayes

For questions and comments about the quality of this book, please contact us at CustomerService@Harlequin.com.

Harlequin Enterprises ULC
22 Adelaide St. West, 41st Floor
Toronto, Ontario M5H 4E3, Canada
www.Harlequin.com

Printed in U.S.A.

After ten years as a television camerawoman, **Ella Hayes** started her own photography business so that she could work around the demands of her young family. As an award-winning wedding photographer, she's documented hundreds of love stories in beautiful locations, both at home and abroad. She lives in central Scotland with her husband and two grown-up sons. She loves reading, traveling with her camera, running and great coffee.

Books by Ella Hayes

Harlequin Romance

Her Brooding Scottish Heir
Italian Summer with the Single Dad
Unlocking the Tycoon's Heart
Tycoon's Unexpected Caribbean Fling
The Single Dad's Christmas Proposal
Their Surprise Safari Reunion
Barcelona Fling with a Secret Prince

Visit the Author Profile page
at Harlequin.com.

This is for all the friends who have supported me on my writing journey. You know who you are. Also, this book goes to my "Cannes Steps" sisters: Elvia, Esme and Dani.

Praise for
Ella Hayes

"Ella Hayes has surpassed herself with this delightfully warm romance. It keeps a reader on their toes with its twists and turns. The characters are believable and you can actually visualize the scenes through the exquisite descriptions. This book ambushes your senses and takes the reader on a beautiful journey with heart-stopping moments. A wonderful relaxing read."

—*Goodreads* on *Italian Summer with the Single Dad*

CHAPTER ONE

The present...

'JULES, PLEASE! Open the door...'

She felt her heart constricting, a fierce heat seizing her throat, aching behind her lids. Why wasn't he taking no for an answer? Why was he torturing her like this?

She swallowed hard, steeling herself. 'Go away, Alden.'

She was trying to hold it in, but it was no good. She could feel her heart tearing, ripping at the seams, tears sliding down her cheeks.

In all the years they had known each other she'd never told him to go away, and it cut like a knife, stung like blazes, but she wasn't opening that door just because suddenly he was on the other side of it.

Did he really expect her to fling it open, smiling, after taking off like that, after abandoning her in Cannes with nothing but a kiss on the forehead, and that splintered whisper that might have been, 'Sorry,' but could have been a dream because she'd been floating at the edges, too sleep-dazed to grasp what was happening?

Until she did. Alden. Gone. No explanation. No 'Sorry, Jules, but they want me in Cairo a day earlier'—which was what she'd told Franc. It was where he'd been, all right. His agent, Jacklyn, had confirmed it. A city with a phone network. Internet! No excuse for not returning her calls, responding to her frantic messages.

Five whole days of heartbreak. Five whole days of nothing but empty, aching silence.

Until this morning. Call after call after call. What she'd wanted for days, but the bruise inside wouldn't let her swipe right. She'd wanted to bruise him back, wanted him to be the one left dangling for once in his life.

Because, the thing was, she always picked up, didn't she? Even when he was on the other side of the world, calling in the wee small hours because he'd forgotten about the time difference, she was always happy to hear his voice because he was her best friend. Even at stupid o'clock in the morning, when every fibre of her being was craving sleep, she *wanted* to hear his news, wanted to feel her lips curving and her belly vibrating, because no one could make her laugh the way Alden could.

But she wasn't laughing now. She was broken because of him. And there he was on the other side of that door, wanting her to let him in, wanting her to…what…forgive him?

'Jules…' There was a heavy thud, as if a hold-all had been dropped. 'I'm not leaving. I'm setting up camp right here.' And then there was a single hard thud on the door—his forehead. 'I'm sorry. Really, really, sorry. Please, Jules, please open the door…'

She felt a fresh scald prickling behind her lids. His voice was stretched tight now, not the kind of tight it was when one of his auditions didn't go well. He always managed to paint over that kind with a pale shade of merry bravado. This was the same kind of strangled, urgent choke that filled his voice when he was talking about his parents—about their refusal to accept that he didn't want to be a surgeon like them, like his brother and sister were, like his grandfather had been—their refusal to approve of him, to concede that acting, not medicine, was his life.

You get me, Jules, so why don't they?

Her heart twisted.

She'd *thought* she got him, but maybe she'd just indulged him because of that irresistible twinkle in his eyes, because of that amusing way he had of talking all the time, of taking himself apart, searching for the truth shard that could explain himself to himself.

All those late-night calls, listening to him pouring his heart out over this lover or that lover—

how they were perfect, then not. She had always taken his side. And after his first few movies, when the press had started seizing on his love life, daubing him a playboy, she'd taken his side too—told him they didn't know what they were talking about—and she'd meant every word.

Because to *her* he had never been flimsy. He'd been warm, dependable. Always there for her. Like when Mum had taken off with that man she'd met at a conference…

She'd been fifteen, hurt, angry, struggling to cope with Dad, who'd been in tatters. And she'd struggled to focus on schoolwork, panicking about exams. And her sister, Emily, had just started uni, so wasn't around to help. But Alden was. He'd got her through it, coming over so they could revise together, shoring her up with moral support and mugs of terrible tea.

And, every time a boyfriend broke her heart, Alden was there like a shot. When Sam had slammed out of the door four months ago, and she'd called him to say she was contemplating a bottle of tequila, he'd told his director he had a family emergency and had come right over.

And, like the consummate actor he was, he'd delivered all the right lines. Sam was a jerk for leaving. Sam was a jerk, full-stop. He'd never liked him—*hated* him, in fact. She was too good for Sam. In fact, she might as well know that, as far as he was concerned, she was too good for

every single one of the boyfriends she'd ever had!
She'd clapped then, laughing and crying at the
same time. Award-winning performance, much!

And later, when her stomach had rebelled, he'd
held her hair back until she was done, then made
her cup after cup of terrible coffee, finally cradling her to sleep on his lap.

That was the Alden she knew. Solid. Kind.
Infinitely warm. But also chronically insecure,
searching for love-slash-approval from someone who mattered, trying so hard to find it that
maybe he *had* developed a tendency to fancy
himself in love when he wasn't really. And
maybe, because of that, he'd bruised some hearts,
but Alden didn't *mean* to hurt anyone. He didn't
have it in him…

That was what she'd thought.

She felt a sob rising. But what to think now?
She'd thought they were in love; thought that
what they'd revealed and shared that last night
in Cannes was real. It had *felt* real—pure, true.
It had felt *meant!* And, if for some reason he'd
got cold feet, then the right way to deal with it,
the right way, would have been to wake up beside her and talk about it like an adult—not van-
ish into the pale blue yonder when she was only
half-conscious.

How could he have done that when he knew
first-hand what Mum's sudden flight had cost
her, done to her?

Oh, but even so, she'd made excuses for him, hadn't she? To save herself from embarrassment, yes, but also to keep up the ruse so as not to let him down, so that he'd still have a chance at the coveted role that had put them on this treacherous path in the first place.

She swallowed hard. Indulging him to the last, even after he'd wronged her so spectacularly, indulging him because she couldn't not. Because she loved him. Always had. And maybe he had a reason for doing what he'd done but she didn't want to hear it. *Couldn't.* He'd trampled her love, shattered her trust.

And now, somehow, he was on the other side of that door—rehearsing his apology, no doubt, getting his lines down, gestures, phrasing, finding his motivation.

She felt her jaw tightening. That would be smoothing things over, of course, rowing them back into the friend zone because he needed her, didn't he, to keep on indulging him, supporting him, plugging the gap his parents weren't filling?

Her heart clenched. Too late! Whatever he was hoping for, she couldn't rewind. If it were possible, she'd have done it already. She would have flat-out refused to go with him to Franc's party and she definitely, definitely, wouldn't have told Franc that she was his fiancée…

CHAPTER TWO

Three weeks earlier...

'THERE MUST BE someone else you can ask?'

Exactly the reaction he'd expected, because Jules didn't feel comfortable with his professional circle, but this was an emergency. Desperate times and all that.

'No, actually, there isn't.'

Her hands stilled around the bouquet she was tying and then she looked up, frowning, her insanely mobile eyebrows going through their familiar moves. 'But you're *Alden Phillips*, not Billy No Mates. You must have a little black book somewhere full of willing victims…?'

'Victims?' He pressed a hand to his heart, conjuring the expected look of deep affront. 'Nice!'

The corner of her mouth ticked up and then she removed her gaze from his, turning back to the flowers.

'What about Celia?'

He felt his own eyebrows drawing in. 'Who?'

'Celia the extra! The one you felt a connection with by the catering van three weeks ago... Blonde hair, violet eyes, sweet pout...'

'Ah...' The girl's face shimmered briefly into view then faded. 'I don't want to take a date, especially someone I hardly know. I'd have to talk to her, look after her, and that's not the point.'

'Whereas if I go you can leave me to my own devices and concentrate on schmoozing your new best friend, Franc Abdali?'

His heart flinched. She was teasing, of course, but still, there was a mystifying little undercurrent in her voice that was tugging at all the old susceptibilities. It happened from time to time, catching him out, but this wasn't the moment to be digging into it. He needed to focus.

'I wouldn't leave you to your own devices—and Franc isn't my *new best friend*—but I need to present well. You know how important this is...'

He could still hardly believe he'd been cast in a Franc Abdali film. It was huge! A massive coup. Franc's films were impeccable. Considered. Nuanced. They were award magnets. What was more, *this* film was an adaptation of his all-time favourite book, *The Darkness of Shadows*. He'd read it so many times, his copy was trashed.

He'd been cast in a supporting role, but it was a pivotal one. A chance to shine, to show the world that he had depth, range, subtlety. Crucially, it was the kind of opportunity that might, finally, earn him some acknowledgement from his parents. A bit of respect instead of the habitual faint disappointment. But there were hurdles to clear first, and he couldn't clear them alone.

He shifted on his feet, trying to draw Jules's gaze. 'I've told you before, Franc is a complicated character...'

'Because of his childhood.' Her eyes flicked up, serious now. 'Because they were refugees.'

'Yes. He saw his father being murdered in Afghanistan, along with his two younger brothers. He escaped with his mother, who had breast cancer, looking after her, carrying her on his back when she was too weak to walk. Eventually they made it to France—'

'Where he procured successful treatment for her, continued his education, got himself into filmmaking, quickly earning worldwide plaudits for his sensitive treatment of difficult subjects...' Her chin dipped. 'I *do* listen, you know.'

Which was why he loved talking to her. So many people only ever half-listened, but Jules took everything in. She was the sponge to his dripping tap, deserved a medal for it, frankly.

But now she was frowning again.

'What I don't understand is why you need a wing person.' She lifted up the bouquet, scrutinising it from every angle, then set it down again. 'I mean, you went to the casting *alone*, got the part... Hooray, hooray.' She mimed a burst of rapturous applause then smiled. 'Done deal, isn't it?'

He felt his ribs tightening, gloom descending.

'I'd thought so, yes, but Jacklyn called earlier. There's been a complication…'

'What kind of complication?'

She was looking at him intently, the concern in her eyes giving way to a familiar protective gleam.

'Apparently Gabriella Perez has pulled out and her role has been filled by—'

'Oh God, don't tell me!' she cut in, shaking her head. 'If it's a complication, then it can only be Natasha Forbes.'

'Yep.'

She let out a long, wavy sigh. 'And I suppose Franc's looking to your agent for reassurance that *that* won't be a problem?'

'More or less.'

Her gaze fell and then she smoothed her hands down her apron, wiping the dampness off. 'And will it?' Her eyes came to his, searching. 'Be a problem, I mean…'

His heart kicked. 'No!'

How could Jules, of all people, be asking him that…? Hadn't he sat upstairs in her flat just six months ago, unpacking the whole Alden-Natasha disaster down to the minutest detail, while she'd plied him with mugs of tea and those delicious butter biscuits she made? Hadn't he, just moments ago, been considering how good a listener she was, how good at remembering?

Maybe he'd been yammering on too much that particular day and she'd tuned out to save her own sanity. Fair enough! But she was listening now—keenly, it seemed—so there was no harm in reiterating.

He tightened his gaze on hers. 'You know I don't have feelings for her any more.'

'Okay.' A smile touched her lips but then it was fading. 'Still, you might find that working with her again could trigger—'

'It won't!'

'How do you know?' She lifted the bouquet, carrying it to a waiting bucket at the furthest end of the work bench. 'You're always talking about the hothouse atmosphere on set…'

He ground his jaw. Why wasn't she letting this go? For sure, he had probably been *more* smitten with Natasha than any other woman he'd ever fallen for, and poor Jules had definitely borne the brunt of it, but if Tash crossed his mind now, she crossed it without a ripple. There was no accompanying tingle, no little lurch of the heart. That was how he knew that working with her again would be fine.

'Jules…?'

Her eyes were down, concentrating on the careful process of lodging the astonishing flower arrangement into its receptacle.

He moved along the bench to where she was. 'Look, be cynical if you must, but I know what I know. It's not going to be an issue.'

Her deft hands stilled for a beat, then carried on with their green-fingered ministrations. Clearly, she wasn't convinced, and was using her silence to declare it. Well, that was fine. He had no problem filling a silence.

'The thing is, Franc doesn't know that, so I need to *show* him. Convince him! His aversion to conflict of any kind, particularly on set, is well-documented. He likes his cast to be tight, like a family, likes his actors to feed off each other artistically, and it obviously works because his films hit the sweet spot every time.'

Jules stepped back from the flowers, folding her arms, and then her eyes lifted. 'And you think you can show him how *over* Natasha you are at a party?' And then her expression was altering, the penny dropping. 'Ah...' She blinked a slow blink. 'Natasha's going to be there, isn't she?'

He felt the tips of his ears growing suddenly, inexplicably, warm. 'Yes.'

'Hmm.' She drew a short, dismissive-sounding breath and then her gaze levelled. 'So isn't that actually perfect, though? I mean, can't you and Natasha buddy up? *Show* Franc that you're oh so professional and completely cool about working together again? That would do the trick, surely? You don't need me.'

He felt his heart flailing against his chest. What was with Jules today, needling him like this? Or maybe he was just predisposed to being needled because Jacklyn's call had knocked him sideways, bringing everything inside to a desperate boil. The thing was, there was so much more to this than Natasha.

'For God's sake, Jules! I've got a chance here… A chance to become Alden Phillips, *actor*, instead of Alden Phillips, heartbreaker. Right now my off-screen reputation is bigger than my bloody career. I get why that's happened because, yes, you're right, the atmosphere on set can make you think things, make you fall for the wrong people. And hands up, for reasons I don't understand I'm the world's worst for doing that, but *you* know better than anyone that there's more to me…'

Her chin lifted a little, acknowledging, and suddenly he was unspooling.

'You, of all people, know how hard I've worked, how much I want to be taken seriously. You know how I love the process of turning lines on the page into a living, breathing character, how I love cinema! The *good* stuff…'

A familiar pale amusement lit her eyes and suddenly a memory flashed. Curtains drawn, both of them sprawled on his bed, propped on pillows. No talking—*his* rule—just watching.

Light flickering on her face, that apple-shampoo scent of her, or maybe it was soap…

He shook himself. 'I mean, you were right there, watching with me: David Lean, Jean-Luc Godard, Ridley Scott, Tarantino… *Calibre* directors. And Franc's in that club, Jules. If this works out, then everything changes for me. I'll be where I want to be.' He felt a nick of bitterness. 'Hell, if I do this well, even my parents might concede that I can act!'

'Oh, Alden…' She was chewing the edge of her lip now, which meant that she was feeling him, empathising, and maybe—just maybe— beginning to cave.

One more push…

'The thing is, I know where I stand in the pecking order and it's way lower than Tash. She's top billing, and I'm the risk, so if there's a shred of doubt hanging over me then I'll be the one who's "released" from contract, not her.

'And, yes, it *is* only a party, but the fact is Franc *did* call my agent. He's concerned, which means he's bound to be watching me, looking for messy remnants…'

Not that he would find any. Tash had dumped him because apparently, he hadn't made her feel *loved* enough, even when he'd been pouring his heart and soul into her, running around after her, giving her his all. He'd bent over backwards, trying to please her. But then it had been, *Alden, I*

*love you, but you don't love me. I think, maybe,
that you're incapable of love.*

Crushing. Beyond painful.

And Jules had been there for him, lending him
her ear, giving him her time. As always.

But the pain he'd felt wasn't heartbreak. He
knew that now, knew that Tash had been right
about the depth of his feelings. It had been an
intense infatuation at best, freighted with hope
and longing—with desperation to prove himself,
maybe, but nothing more.

No, the real pain had come from the tender
nerve she'd struck with that whole 'incapable of
love' thing. Because it bothered him that all his
relationships withered, that he could never seem
to find...

He pushed the thought away. No messy remnants! That was the point to prove, and he could,
easily. But, just in case Natasha was harbouring
resentment—or, God help him, looking to go a
second round—he needed a shield.

He drew Jules back into focus. 'I need an ally,
Jules. A friend.' He felt his hand lifting involun-
tarily in her direction. 'My best friend.'

Her eyes held him for a long second and then
they were narrowing. 'But you're not asking me
to go as your *best friend*, are you? Not if you're
trying to convince Franc that he doesn't need to
worry about you and Natasha.'

Three steps ahead, as always.

He let his hand fall. 'I was going to get to that.'

Her arms tightened across her front. 'You want me to hold your hand *literally*, don't you? You want me to pretend I'm your girlfriend, spend the night looking at you adoringly.'

'I know it's a big ask…'

Was that a twitch affecting the side of her mouth? He felt hope jumping. 'Do you think you could manage it?' A spark of mischief. 'If it's any consolation, it would be quite a stretch for me too, having to look at you fondly.'

She shot him a wide, withering smile but then her eyes turned serious. 'I don't see how it can work, though. I mean, Franc might fall for it, but Natasha *knows* I'm a friend of yours, right?'

'No…' Which, saying out loud, sounded strange even to his own ears, but it was the truth. 'I mean, she knows I have friends but, sick as it sounds, we were so into each other that we didn't get into that many nuts and bolts…'

'Hmm.' Her eyebrows went up with an air of derision. 'Well, speaking as chief nut, I'm still not convinced your plan has legs because I'm a florist, not Greta Garbo. Besides—' her eyes clouded '—you know I'd feel awkward and out of place…'

She licked her lips, as if she was going to add something, but then she seemed to change her mind. She gave a little shrug. 'You know I didn't much like the drama crowd you hung out with at school.'

'Well, some of them weren't very likeable, so fair play.'

Her mouth twisted into a reluctant smile, warming him inside. Jules's smile never grew old. If only she would use it more, let herself go with people a bit, but it seemed so hard for her.

His stomach clenched. Her mother Paulina's fault for leaving like that, without warning! Jules had always held part of herself in after that. Except with him. And with her boyfriends. Probably.

He refocused. 'Look, if it helps, it's going to be quite a small affair, so not too many luvvies for you to contend with. And Franc is charming, not full of himself or anything. I think you'd like him.'

'I might.' Her head was tilting over, her eyes teasing now. 'That's *if* I agree to this ridiculous ruse.'

If...

He felt a smile tugging. The thing about Jules was that she couldn't keep her thoughts out of her eyes. The decision was already made and shining through the startling blue. She *was* coming! She was going to save his miserable tush by pretending to be his besotted girlfriend.

He sucked his smile back down and swallowed. He mustn't let her see that he was already popping corks inside. Better to spin it out, beg a little, so she could feel all the power.

He clapped a hand over his heart. 'Pretty please, Jules. Be my party girl, just for one night. In return, I promise you lifelong fealty. Undying gratitude. I also promise to thank you first when I collect my award for best supporting actor...'

Her eyebrows slid up to maximum elevation. 'Oh, you'll do more than that, Alden Phillips. I expect a long, effusive, over-egged monologue with tears—*lots* of tears—and, let me see, a couple of loud, gulpy sobs.' She unfolded her arms and then she was stretching out a hand towards him across the bench. 'Deal?'

He felt his heart exploding, a smile breaking loose and wide. With Jules beside him, he couldn't fail. With Jules beside him, everything was going to work out.

He put his hand in hers and shook. 'Deal.'

CHAPTER THREE

'Look at it this way.' Alden hit the indicator, slowing for the turning. 'It's a talking point; gives you the chance to tell people what you do.'

'You'll be suggesting I hand out business cards next.'

He glanced over. 'That's not a bad idea, actually. Think of all those opening night bouquets—and what about awards dinners? Table centrepieces! It's a massive market, and that's not even counting the private soirees like tonight's. You could make a killing.'

Was he serious? Hard to tell when he was excitable like this, talking over his nerves to stop himself from feeling them.

One thing for sure, it was a pointless conversation because she had no intention of pushing her floristry business at Franc Abdali's little party, even if the hospital bandage binding her left wrist from forearm to hand *was* a prompt. It wasn't as if she'd sprained it doing anything worth talking about! Just a stupid altercation with a stepladder at the wedding venue she had been dressing that morning. One missed rung, one mighty tumble, and now…

Her belly clenched. Now she was going to be doubly conspicuous. Not only would she be entering a room full of luvvies on Alden's arm but sporting a beacon-bright bandage into the bargain. And to think that he had bought her the navy dress because she'd wanted to look understated!

She fingered the soft silk folds in her lap and then, in spite of herself, she could feel a smile coming. The day after she'd agreed to be his fake date, he'd dragged her out, chivvying her along New Bond Street saying he owed her a dress at least. Even though she'd told him she had plenty of dresses, he'd seemed so delighted by the prospect of kitting her out that, while it had felt a little weird—well, *seriously* weird, actually—she'd gone along with it.

And then, in the fitting rooms at Elinor Brown—maybe because she'd still been as stiff as dry grass—he'd started riffing *Pretty Woman* base beats on his air guitar, cajoling her into performing each dress, strutting, catwalk-style, drawing the clown out of her until they both couldn't breathe for laughing.

They'd ended up with two contenders. Alden had liked the red one, and so had she, secretly, but it was cut too low, split too high. She hadn't felt confident enough to choose it.

She flicked him a glance. He was always telling her to be more confident, to believe in herself. But then, she was always saying the same thing to him too. And they *did* believe to a point; they must do because they *were* both successful…to a point.

He *was* making movies, even if they weren't the ones he wanted to make. And Wild Blooms *was* doing well, even if her clients were still mostly opting for traditional blooms rather than the wild, *avant-garde* arrangements she wanted to do.

So, they weren't an utterly hopeless pair, but they both had an unquenched part. And now Alden was within touching distance. This party was his last hurdle, a leap towards the career he wanted.

And she wanted it for him, wanted him to be happy and satisfied, because he'd worked so damn hard for it. And, if he got himself onto that hallowed ground, then maybe his parents would stop piling on the silent disappointment and see him for the shining star he was. She wanted that for him, and more. It was why she was here, putting herself through this, putting herself on parade in front of the loathsome Natasha Forbes!

Her stomach dipped. Oh, God, and that was why she should have picked the red dress! Why hadn't she? Too busy thinking about herself, her own stupid shyness, instead of seeing what Alden had clearly seen but hadn't pressed upon her because he was too freaking nice!

Walking into the party on his arm in *that* dress would have made a statement, a resounding declaration. One glance and Franc's concerns would have dissolved. That dress could have spoken for her, would have shown all and sundry—*Natasha*—that she was confident in herself and in her 'relationship' with Alden. By implication, he would have appeared solid—a risk-free, safe bet!

In the demure navy silk she was going to have to work at it, rely on her personality and non-existent acting skills, to convince a room full of people she didn't know, couldn't imagine herself ever wanting to know, that she was Alden's latest love interest.

She shuddered, touching her wrist. And now, to crown it all, there was this bloody bandage.

'Is it hurting terribly, darling?'

He was doing his stage voice, shooting her a merry look.

She bit into her smile to stop it spreading, loading her voice with passionate stoicism. 'A little. But I shall endure it for your sake, my love.'

He laughed. 'There you go. Every inch Greta Garbo!'

'If only!'

He turned his gaze back to the road. 'You'll be fine.'

Was he trying to reassure her or himself? He sounded confident, but it wasn't as if they'd rehearsed, practised any little intimacies. For some reason they'd avoided that conversation, probably because of the weirdness, but now she was regretting it. She was going in blind. All right for Alden: he was an actor. He could slip his skin in a moment, turn himself into someone else. It was what he did the moment he was with his set…

Her stomach squirmed. It was the thing she was most dreading about tonight—that he would become this unrecognisable person and that she would be alone, *feel* alone, even holding his hand.

And she'd wanted to say it to him the other day in her work room, but then she'd stopped herself, fallen back on the old chestnut of how she didn't feel comfortable with the acting fraternity. Because telling him the truth, that what made her uncomfortable was the way he could be when he was with them, would only have thrown him into one of his spirals.

She bit her lips together. That old chestnut had kept her safe for years, fencing her off from his alien side, but there would be no fence tonight. God help her, she was going to be there with him on *his* side, pretending to be his lovestruck girlfriend.

Lovestruck…

She looked over. His face was flashing pale in the headlights of the oncoming cars. A nice face. A dear face. Prone to smiling at the drop of a hat, one of those electric smiles that made your heart fall out even when you were only a friend.

She felt her heart pause. When they were sixteen, she'd sometimes imagined she could feel a little current travelling between them. Or perhaps it had been in her head because she was hurting over Mum, and he'd used to come over and help her with her homework, sitting close, being kind. Whatever! She'd felt little flutters in her belly, little tingles shuttling up and down her spine.

She looked away, felt her ribs tightening. The day Sam left, she'd felt those same tingles rippling again, hadn't she, shimmering through the tequila fog, through the haze of warmth and peace inside Alden's arms. Illicit flutterings, intimate stirrings she'd had no business entertaining. Feelings that she'd forced off stage, stashed, stowed, dumped, because Alden was her friend. Her best friend…

But *those* were the feelings she needed to resurrect tonight, put to work so she could pull this whole thing off. It was a matter of committing to the role, putting everything into it, being confident.

She flexed the fingers of her left hand. She had to be confident, forget about the dress and the bandage because this was about Alden. His Best

Supporting Actor award was hanging in the balance, after all. And, if she needed an extra incentive, she only had to think about Natasha Forbes, telling Alden he was incapable of love, hurting him like that!

She felt her jaw tightening. Ms Forbes could do with being taught a lesson, and she was more than ready to step up and deliver it. Might be rather fun to show Natasha how wrong she was. How very, very wrong.

CHAPTER FOUR

'I THOUGHT YOU said it was going to be a *small* party...'

Jules was hissing panic into his ear, and no wonder! The hotel suite they'd just walked into was teeming. Familiar faces. Unfamiliar. A throng!

And then his heart clenched. Oh, God! How could he have been so dim? There was Sylvia Dent, and Chris Bratt, and Joe Rubens. This was clearly Franc's premiere party for the cast and crew of his new film, *Slowcoach*. Franc must have invited him, and the other principal *Darkness* actors, along as a friendly gesture. And, of course, Franc *would* be hosting it ahead of the actual screening in Leicester Square tomorrow night because he was jetting off to Los Angeles straight after the premiere, wasn't he? To finalise the production budget for *Darkness*.

It was all coming back now...

After that last screen test a fortnight ago, Franc had been complaining to him about production hold-ups that had left his current schedule jammed. He'd said he was sick of tearing around and that he couldn't wait for the following week, when they'd all be coming together at his mansion in Cannes for the script read through.

Jacklyn must have got her wires crossed somehow, confusing the small party of cast members bound for Cannes with tonight's grand party. He could handle it, but Jules was busy having a meltdown.

He bent to her ear. 'I'm sorry. Jacklyn said that…' And then suddenly there was a prickle starting at the back of his neck. They were being noticed. Watched. *Evaluated.* He could feel eyes burning into him, like in those first few moments on stage before you spoke your opening line. Eyes burning, noting the stiffness between Jules and him.

Not the impression he'd been going for.

He straightened, loosening off his shoulders, then lifted his hand to tuck a stray curl behind her ear.

Her eyes flew wide. 'What are you doing?'

If they hadn't been standing on the threshold of Franc's hotel suite in front of a hundred-odd people, the shock on her face would have made him laugh out loud. As it was…

'I'm touching you, my darling, and now I'm going to look at you lovingly.'

Come on, Jules!

He smiled, leaning towards her so their foreheads were barely a centimetre apart. 'If you could be so good as to return the favour…'

She made a sudden small, strangled noise of acknowledgement and then her lips were curving sweetly, and her eyes were rounding into his.

'Of course, my love.' Her right hand came up, covering his for a long second, and then she drew it down firmly, squeezing hard. 'But please don't touch my hair. You paid Gerard a lot of money to make it look this good. If you mess it up, I can't fix it with just the one hand.'

Merriness in her eyes, shot through with a warning.

He felt his heart wilt. They should have rehearsed this stuff, practised some small loving gestures, but he hadn't wanted to suggest it because this was Jules and with Jules there'd always seemed to be a bit of a barrier there, a long-held habit of *not* touching.

The only time that barrier ever crashed was when she was upset, usually over some dolt who didn't deserve to kiss her feet. *Then* she would fall into his arms, crying into his shirt, sometimes laying her head in his lap and letting him stroke her hair until she was all cried out. But now her hair was off-limits.

He shook himself. As it should be, because she was right—if he inadvertently dislodged a pin, she wouldn't be able to fix it herself. It was why he'd called in Gerard in the first place. And Gerard had done a fine job. Her hair looked nice, *appropriate*, all sleekly swept up, although—no disrespect to Gerard—he preferred it the way she usually wore it, a twisted-up chaos of brown curls with a pencil stuck through.

'I'm sorry.' He moved his hand, wrapping it around hers, giving it a squeeze. 'I wasn't thinking.'

Her eyebrows twitched. 'Too lovestruck, I suppose?'

He felt a smile coming, a proper one this time, because the warning was gone, replaced by the all too familiar sparkling mischief.

'Oh, my sweet darling, you have no idea...'

Did he dare to kiss her on the forehead? Their audience would lap it up for sure and wasn't that the whole point of her being here—to show how devoted to her he was, ergo how over Natasha he was? And surely she wouldn't rear back, not now that they were in the zone, twinkling at each other? *Acting!* The thing was *not* to lunge.

He squeezed her hand again, then leaned towards her, pausing for a beat so she would get his drift, and then he pressed his lips to her hairline. 'Truth to tell, I'm in so deep right now that I'm struggling to breathe.'

A small, snorting noise erupted from her nose and then she was leaning away a little, eyes dancing. 'That sounds quite alarming. Do you need to sit down, put your head between your knees?'

'I'm not that flexible.'

In one fluid movement her eyebrows drew in then lifted. 'Oh, ElastiMan, that's simply not true.'

He felt a chuckle vibrating. *Trust her!* Elasti-Man had been his first professional voiceover part. Just a segment in a TV show for the under-fives, which he'd blagged his way into somehow during his first year at RADA. But Jules had declared it a vindication of his decision to quit medical school for acting and treated him to a bottle of victory champagne she couldn't really afford. They'd drunk it in Richmond Park. Paper cups. Blanket on the ground. Sunshine warming their backs. She'd told him to keep the cork as a memento, which he did. It was still in a drawer somewhere…

He raised one eyebrow at her. 'Very droll!'

'Well, I'm trying my best, so we look all jolly and loved up.' Her eyes flashed a tease. 'It's bloody hard, though, this acting business, especially when your co-star sucks. I'm exhausted already.'

She looked away, laughing, but then suddenly her gaze was whipping back, locking on tight, a fire behind it that stopped his breath. And then her hand was pulling out of his and before he knew what was happening, she was putting it to his face, stroking her thumb over his cheekbone. 'By the way, have I told you how handsome you look tonight…?'

His heart vaulted into his throat. What was she doing? This didn't feel like acting. Or maybe he'd simply lost the ability to discern fantasy from reality, because her touch was busy rerouting the blood from his brain to his groin.

And then suddenly Natasha's cool voice shattered the moment.

'Alden…'

He inhaled, composing himself, and turned, vaguely aware of Jules's hand on his shoulder blade exerting a small, bolstering pressure.

'Hello, Tash.'

He felt his pulse slowing. Same old Tash. Pale. Lean. Elegant. Her hair was longer now, loose around her shoulders. Her lips were red, her signature shade, but he was happy to note that he had no inclination whatsoever to kiss them. He couldn't not air-kiss her, though, in case Franc was watching from some hidden corner.

He went through the motions. 'How are you?'

'Oh, you know. Fine.' The red lips smiled. 'Looking forward to working together again.' And then her eyes widened. 'You must be thrilled about the Caspar part…'

For a B-grade actor, she might as well have said. Well, he wasn't rising to her bait. Neither could he be bothered to remind her that they had met on the set of *Revolution Day*, a popcorn movie that for some reason—*money*—she had deigned to do.

He smiled. 'Of course I am. Who doesn't want to work with Franc Abdali?' He shifted so he could slide his arm around Jules's waist. 'Tash, this is Jules...' He caught Jules's eye, felt a smile twitching. She was trying not to look openly hostile, failing utterly. 'Jules, this is Natasha Forbes.'

'Nice to meet you, Natasha.' Jules smiled suddenly, as if she'd only just remembered that she could. 'I've heard so *much* about you.'

What?

He clamped her waist tighter, hoping she'd feel the warning in it. Bad enough that Natasha had designated him a fly-by-night. He didn't want her thinking he was the kiss-and-tell type as well, or that she even crossed his mind any more.

'What I meant...' Jules was squirming away from his hand, smiling more widely '...is that your reputation is well-deserved. Not that I'm a pundit or anything, but I do enjoy your films. I especially loved you in *Revolution Day*...'

Oh, no...

Her voice climbed an octave, taking on a bright, tinkly quality. 'Such a *fun* part for you.'

Natasha blinked a little, adjusting the glass in her hand. 'Yes, well, it's important to have a little fun sometimes—show a different side of yourself. Of course, I have to remind myself to do that, whereas Alden...' Her eyes came to his, her mouth twisting into an odd, slanted smile. 'You've got an enviable talent for not taking anything, or *anyone*, too seriously, haven't you?'

The same old barb. That he was only out for fun, that he was *incapable* of love.

Why was she taunting him about it now? Wasn't she over it—*them*—past caring, like him? Or maybe it was for Jules's benefit—a little poison dart to pay her back for the *Revolution Day* quip, to seed some doubt in her mind about what kind of man he was, stir up a bit of disharmony between them. Obviously, *that* wasn't going to work, but there was certainly something stirring in Jules. He could feel her bristling hard against him.

He shrugged. 'I don't know if I'd call it a talent, Tash. It's just what's been required in the movies I've done so far. It's why I'm so excited to be working with Franc. Finally I've got a chance to show that I have a different side too.'

Natasha's gaze flickered, registering the deliberate disingenuousness. Was she registering the subtext too: that he didn't want to be grinding old axes; that he wanted them to move on, *get on* with each other professionally, enjoy working together on *Darkness*?

He shot her a smile, loading his gaze with as much warmth as he could muster so she would know that he wasn't holding onto any bitterness, and then he looked up, scanning the room. 'Speaking of Franc, have you seen him? We really need to go and say hello.'

For a long second, he could feel Natasha's eyes burning into him and then she turned, pointing towards the bar. 'Yes. He was over there the last time I saw him, talking to Hayden.'

Alden lifted two flutes off a passing tray and put one into her hand. 'Here you go. You probably need it after that!'

After meeting Natasha, he was clearly trying not to say, but it was all over his face.

'That would be a resounding yes.' She touched her glass to his, resisting the urge to grimace. 'Thank you.'

'No, thank *you*.' He smiled and then he was leaning in close, whispering, 'For coming. For propping me up.'

She felt her heart giving, then a sudden swirling chaos. All this warm proximity was stirring her senses up. The way his hair was tickling her head right now, the warmth of his palm against hers before, that warm pressure of his lips on her forehead earlier.

Not worth thinking about, because it was only acting, but at the same time it was impossible not to think about it because being this close felt nice. Being touched by him felt nice. Strange, too, but in a good way. All in all, confusing.

Was he feeling confused?

She stepped back so she could see his face,

going for playfulness. 'Oh, you know, darling—anything for you.'

His eyes lit, registering the quip, and then he turned his gaze to the wider room, looking for Franc.

She put her glass to her lips. Nothing in his expression to go on other than that he was pre-occupied. So maybe it was just her, then, flailing around inside, feeling hyper-aware.

She sipped again, feeling the first inklings of a champagne buzz, the small loosening effect.

One thing for sure: stroking his face had patently weirded him out but she'd had no choice. Natasha had been slithering over in her silver satin, long, red talons flashing, smiling with that big red mouth of hers. She couldn't help herself. The woman had hurt him—told him he was incapable of love! She'd wanted to give Ms Forbes something meaty to feast on. Besides, it was what she'd come for, wasn't it—to *adore* Alden, to be his girlfriend for the night?

'By the way, super-subtle of you, mentioning *Revolution Day* like that…'

His gaze swung back: deep, blue, a little bit devastating.

She felt the chaos swirling again and took another sip to reset. 'I didn't think we were doing subtlety. Besides, *she* started it.' She couldn't stop herself from mimicking Natasha's wide eyes and low drawl. 'You must be *thrilled* about the Caspar part.'

The corner of his mouth ticked up, the way it did when he was trying to stop himself from smiling.

'I mean *that* was hardly subtle of *her*, was it?'

'No, I suppose not.' And then his gaze darted to her left wrist. 'How are you holding up, by the way? Is it hurting?'

Her heart squeezed. He was in caring mode, wrapping her up in that invisible blanket of his, the one he always pulled out when she was sad or sore. He had so many modes and she knew all of them. Well, nearly all of them. Natasha Forbes would know a few different ones.

'It's fine, thanks. I can barely hear it throbbing over this noise.'

He cracked his electric smile and then his hand was sliding around her waist, clearly still mindful of the illusion they were selling. 'Right, then. If you're okay to proceed, we need to find Fra—'

'Alden!'

Her breath caught. Joe Rubens—the living, breathing, multi-award-winning Joe Rubens— was intercepting them.

'Joe!' Alden released her and in the next moment he was pumping Joe's hand warmly. 'How's it going?'

'Good, obviously!' Joe smiled and then he leaned forward, sweeping a hand through his blond mop. 'Although, between you and me, I'm sick to death of the bloody press interviews. *Slow-coach* is a stunning film, but I mean, how many times can you say it?'

Alden was nodding, squaring his shoulders, sliding into that alien skin of his. 'Tell me about it. I lose interest in the press stuff about ten minutes in, but hey, look on the bright side—at least *Slowcoach* is a great film…'

Joe laughed, reading the words that Alden wasn't saying—that promoting the kind of movies *he* did was even more of a drag.

She felt her lips pursing. This was what she didn't like about Alden when he was with these people—the way he stood up straight to seem confident then destroyed the whole effect by letting his insecurity hang out like a shirt tail.

Maybe the movies he'd made to date weren't highbrow, but they were entertaining. And Alden had screen presence, charisma in spades, as well as great comic timing. He ought to have been proud of that, owning it.

And, yes, there was more inside him for sure, but it was hard to watch him subtly trashing himself because in some stupid, insecure part of his brain he'd decided that Joe Rubens was better than he was. The infuriating thing was that Joe himself obviously didn't think that. Joe's eyes were full of warmth and admiration.

'God, I'm sorry…' Alden flicked her a glance

and then he was stepping back, reclaiming her waist with a firm hand. 'I'm being unforgivably rude. Joe, this is Jules.'

Joe's famous light-green eyes crinkled in her direction. 'Hi, Jules. Nice to meet you.'

Genuine warmth. No guile.

She felt her smile opening out. 'You too. And congratulations on *Slowcoach*. I can't wait to see it.'

Joe grinned, hamming. 'Well, I'm *brilliant* in it, of course, so, you know, it's worth a watch.' He chuckled roundly and then his eyes fell on the bandage. 'Gosh! Have you been in the wars?'

She smiled. 'More of a minor skirmish. Far too dull to talk about.'

Joe laughed again, and then his eyes slid back to Alden.

Did he want to talk to Alden alone? It seemed that something was gathering behind his eyes, something he wanted to divulge…

She looked at Alden. It would do him good to be taken into Joe's confidence, someone he considered higher up the greasy pole. Because it *was* a greasy pole. A slippery existence. It was why Alden's parents didn't want it for him, but what they wanted shouldn't count, even if they meant well. Acting, not medicine, was Alden's life, the thing he lived and breathed for.

And now Joe seemed to have something to say to him that might be nothing but gossip, but equally could be something important, a tip, and she was in the way.

Her heart pulsed. She didn't want to be in Alden's way. Not now. Not ever.

She looked at Joe then eased herself out of Alden's grip, flashing him what she hoped was an encouraging look. 'I'm sorry, but would you please excuse me? I need to powder my nose.'

There was a faint breeze blowing across the outside terrace which felt like balm after the thick air inside. Not so many guests out here, and no familiar faces, thank God. The journey to the ladies' room had been a non-stop heart-hop, an exercise in not looking dumbly starstruck. This was tranquil, pleasant. The question was, how long to wait before going back in?

She turned, considering the line of full-length windows that looked out over the terrace, then set off along them, looking through, skirting the giant urns of exquisite tree ferns that flanked each elegant window, until she could see Joe's blond head and Alden's sandy one bent together. They were deep in conversation, their faces serious.

A bit longer, then, but that was fine. She liked being in the anonymous darkness, liked watching the headlights and taillights ebbing along the road across the park. It was soothing, mesmerising.

But then, suddenly, there were voices and high-heeled footsteps approaching, drawing nearer until they were stopping right there on the other side of the planter.

Jules bit down hard on her lip. There was no escape, short of popping out and giving the poor women a heart attack. The only option was to stay put and keep quiet.

'So how was it, talking to him again?'

'Tricky.'

Her heart froze. The cool tone of the second voice was instantly recognisable.

'Oh, Natasha, I'm sorry.' A cigarette lighter rasped, followed by a brief inhaling pause. 'Then again, it's been six months. And forgive me for being blunt, but what did you expect? After all, it was *you* who dumped—'

'I know that!' Natasha paused then sighed. 'I just didn't expect him not to come round, not to fight for me.' Another sigh. 'I called him out to wake him the hell up! Get him to, I don't know, *give* himself fully. Is that unreasonable?'

'No.' The friend was being gentler now. 'You loved him. Naturally you wanted all of him.'

'Yeah, instead of the sixty percent I got!'

Sixty?

Jules felt her jaw clenching. One hundred and sixty, more like! The way he used to run around after her, taking the red eye to spend a few precious hours with her when they were filming on opposite sides of the world. What did the woman want—Alden's actual blood?

'Silly, silly, Natasha…' Another long sigh. 'I thought he'd come back, come through with the other forty, but, true to form, he's moved on. Got someone new.'

This was the litmus test. Had she and Alden managed to sell their fake relationship?

The smoker blew out a breathy plume. 'Who is she?'

'Jules… He didn't offer a surname.' Natasha's voice sharpened, shading into cattiness. 'I'll bet he doesn't even know it. She's probably some extra he chatted up by the catering van. One thing's for sure, she's quite the shrew!'

Shrew?

And then Natasha made a derisory little noise. 'Anyway, it won't last.'

'Why?'

'Because he's *Alden Phillips*, of course. But also…' There was a pause and then Natasha's voice took on a smug, knowing quality. 'But also because, just before we said goodbye, he looked at me like he used to—you know? All warm and hungry…'

A shiver sliced across her shoulder blades. *Had* Alden looked at Natasha with hungry eyes? If so, she hadn't caught it!

The smoker's voice dipped low. 'Tash, you can't be thinking…'

'Why not? We're going to be in Cannes next week for one of Franc's famous script sessions, and it's not as if I owe the shrew any favours! I mean, she's just arrived, whereas Alden and I have history, not to mention *intense* sexual chemistry.' She let out a tortured groan. 'God knows, I'm so *horny* right now, I'd totally settle for pure sex. Just the thought of that tight, scrumptious little tush and the way he used to…'

Jules pressed her hands to her ears hard, blocking out the rest. Alden's tush *was* note-worthy—anyone could see that—but she didn't want to hear their bedroom secrets.

And then there was a sudden brisk, back-and-forth scuffing noise: the smoker grinding out her cigarette. 'And on *that* lewd note, I think we should go back inside. I'm freezing.'

'Freezing is the price you pay for smoking.' Natasha's voice was admonishing. 'You really need to give up, Zara. Smoking is *not* cool.'

And then they were on their way, voices and footsteps fading.

She exhaled, loosening off her shoulders. So, Natasha had designs on Alden in spite of this evening's charade. In spite of all the hand holding and touching, the billing and the cooing, all the warm, weird feelings swirling. Nice feelings. Confusing feelings. After going through all that, she was an inconsequential shrew to be batted out of the way because Natasha and Alden had history—not to mention *intense* sexual chemistry! As if anyone wanted to hear about that!

She massaged her wrist. It was probably a lie, anyway; in fact, it was honestly hard to understand how a warm, kind soul like Alden could have fallen for Natasha at all. Granted, appearances could be deceptive. Maybe, privately, Natasha was sweet and loving, but outwardly she seemed cold. *Brittle.* Blessed with a fertile imagination, though, seeing so-called hunger in Alden's eyes.

As if! Hadn't he stood in her work room just two days ago and told her that he didn't have feelings for Natasha any more?

Her belly went cold. And what had she said back to him? That working together again could trigger old desires, old feelings. He'd said it wouldn't but, even if that were true on his part, if Natasha were to start throwing herself at him, however subtly, it was bound to affect his focus. Bound to cause an atmosphere which Franc might interpret as conflict—conflict that Franc might choose to eliminate by axing Alden from the film, the film that was the keystone to everything.

Her heart clopped. She had to tell him! *Warn* him. But not in front of Joe.

Were they still talking?

She turned to look, and her heart seized. Joe was gone, and now Natasha was standing next to

Alden, smiling her wide, flat smile as she chatted to the other man who was standing with them—a serious-looking type, olive skinned, fine-boned, dark eyed.

Franc Abdali!

And she was out here, being of no help whatsoever!

She struck across the terrace, heart drumming. She had to get back to Alden's side. More than ever now, she had to show them all that she and Alden were tight as clams. Solid as a rock. And especially, she had to show Franc that Alden was settled, serious, not going to get himself tangled up with his scheming co-star.

She pushed through the doors, pausing to breathe. She had to render Alden untouchable, somehow, Natasha-proof! The question was, how?

'It won't be *all* work next week, though…' Franc's smile was gentle, weary. 'It's a while since I've been home and I want to rest, meditate, centre myself before everything gets crazy again.' He shrugged an apology. 'Do you mind the prospect of a little down time while you're staying with me?'

Alden smiled. 'Of course not.' Except he did mind. Ever since Natasha had arrived by his side, she'd been touching him, leaning in, standing too close. If this was a foretaste of what it would be like in Cannes…

'Ditto for me, Frankie. I mean, what's not to like about down time, especially on the Riviera?' Natasha's eyes came to his. 'Frankie's villa has the best sea views, Alden.' Her hand settled on his shoulder yet again. 'You're going to love it.'

'I'm sure I will.' He smiled back with warmth, because what else could he do in front of Franc? And then he met Franc's gaze. 'It's very kind of you to host us in your own home.'

'Not at all. It's the best way for us all to bond. It's the way I like to work. I want us to feel like a family, work together as a family.'

His chest went tight. Did Franc have any notion of what might be about to happen to his little family of cast members? Franc was such a nice person that he almost wanted what Joe had just told him about Hayden Coulter not to be true, even though it could open up…

Stop!

Thinking about it now was pointless. Right now, he had bigger fish to fry, such as resisting the impulse to break eye contact with Franc so he could scan the room for Jules.

Where the hell was she? She was supposed to be draping herself over him, convincing Franc that he was demonstrably over Natasha. Meanwhile, Natasha was getting on his nerves, and he was *this* close to cracking, showing that, far from being cool about working with her again, he was—

'Hi, babe!'

Jules!

Here. Gorgeous. A sight for sore eyes!

Could she see his joy leaping, feel the intensity of his relief? He let his breaking smile say it for him. 'I was about to send out a search party.'

'I'm so sorry.' She slid herself in between Natasha and him, kissed him on the cheek, and then she was turning to look at Franc, lifting her injured wrist into view, smiling that sparkly smile of hers. 'Needless to say, visiting the powder room is quite the workout with only one functional hand.'

And then her eyes came back to his for a fleeting moment, a fleeting moment he would replay in his mind later, trying to pin down the exact nanosecond within it when the idea crystallised in her head and turned itself into words.

'You must be Franc Abdali.' She put out her good hand for Franc to shake. 'I'm Jules Beckett— Alden's fiancée.'

CHAPTER FIVE

'I'M SORRY, but I *had* to do something…'

Jules was staring up at him from the passenger seat, her eyes shadowy in the paltry light of the hotel's subterranean carpark.

'Okay…' He shut her door and tailed round to the driver's side, trying to find his feet, his breath, a chink of comprehension.

Engaged was quite the escalation! He'd played along, of course—*acting*—smiling and nodding, because what else could he do? Jules had taken control, chatting away to Franc, pausing to make the occasional smiling face at Natasha.

He'd proposed a week ago, apparently. They were planning to marry next year, maybe in the spring. Jules was hoping for a small ceremony in Florence, because she loved Florence, but of course everything depended on him, on his shooting schedule etcetera.

Franc had clearly been charmed. Natasha, less so. Meanwhile, he was struggling to land a single coherent thought, barrelling as he was through the land of disbelief on his way to the land of monster repercussions. Had she given a thought to those or noticed Franc whispering into his ear as they were saying goodbye?

The thing to do was to stay calm. This was Jules. She must have had a reason.

He slid in behind the wheel and looked over. 'So, why?'

'Because of what I overheard Natasha saying to her friend...'

'In the powder room?'

'No, in the drawing room with a candlestick!' She pulled one of her adorable bug-eyed faces and then she was shaking her head at him. 'On the terrace, if you must know, but please, let me speak!'

He flashed his palms, chastened.

'Okay.' She took a little breath. 'So she said she only dumped you to wake you up; that she wanted all of you, not just the sixty percent she maintains you were giving her. She said she'd wanted you to fight for her, which I think basically means she expected you to come crawling back.'

'After telling me I was *incapable* of love?' He felt the tender nerve twinging. 'Was she serious?'

Jules stared at him. 'Maybe. I don't know. I'm just reporting what she said. In any case, that's not the important bit.' She took a histrionic breath. 'She went on to say that when you're in Cannes she's going to make a play for you. That she'd even settle for a fling…'

He felt a wave of mild revulsion and, close on its heels, a sharp stab of guilt. He'd wanted Tash once, hadn't he? He'd longed for her, loved the thought of being her boyfriend, sold himself on the idea of them. *Oh, God!* He really was fickle. Shallow. Self-absorbed. Every bad thing the press said he was. His heart seized. Maybe he *was* incapable of love…

'Anyway…' Jules was angling herself towards him. 'I *know* you're not interested in her any more, because we've well and truly had *that* conversation, but it came to me that she could still be a distraction because, you know—' her gaze sharpened into his '—you *can* and *do* get distracted when it comes to this kind of thing, and if you do then it could go badly for you, because of the pecking order and everything…' A shadow flitted across her face. 'So I was coming to warn you, but then Natasha was already there, pawing at you, and all I could think was that I *had* to save you. I just didn't know how until suddenly, when I was showing Franc my wrist, it came to me. My hand was covered up. No one would be able to see that I wasn't wearing a ring.'

Faultless thinking in the circumstances. A genius solution.

Almost…

'That's why I did it.' She let out an accomplished little sigh. 'So now, when you go, you'll be going as an engaged man. Natasha won't dare touch you, and you'll be able to focus on what you're doing, and Franc will be happy. And then after you've finished shooting the film, at some convenient later moment, you can simply…' She circled her good hand in a prompting gesture.

'Let it be known that we've broken things off?'

'Exactly.' She shrugged, gave a little smile. 'And it'll be fine. It's not as if anyone will be shocked that things didn't work out.'

'Because that's the way all my relationships go!' He felt stung, couldn't hide it. 'Thanks a lot, Jules!'

Her mouth stiffened. 'Hey, come on… You know I didn't mean…' And then she was shaking her head, frowning at him, stirring the old susceptibilities around. 'I'm only saying what you say yourself all the time—that your relationships don't last.'

He looked away, heart drumming. She was right. He did say it all the time, bored her rigid with it probably, because he couldn't understand why his relationships always bombed.

He wasn't scared of love, like most of the characters he played were. He put himself out there— *tried*—but things always seemed to fizzle out, as if there wasn't enough plot to carry the story. Time after time. And now he had a reputation that didn't fit with who he was inside: the person

Jules knew. Maybe that was why hearing her say it hurt. It was a crushing thought that even she could be starting to lose sight of him.

He forced his eyes back to hers. 'I'm sorry. I'm being stupidly sensitive.' Her gaze softened and he felt his insecurities responding, gathering, spilling out before he could stop them. 'And I know you meant well, diving in to save me, and I'm not blaming you at all, okay? But the stupidly sensitive part of me can't help thinking that this is only going to add fuel to the fire.'

Her forehead crimped. 'What do you mean?'

'Well, it isn't *just* a relationship this time, is it? It's an engagement. When it all goes tits up, it'll be, "surprise, surprise: playboy Phillips successfully dodges altar!". Or maybe they'll go for outright comedy: "will someone—anyone!—please take this man?"'

'Stop it!' She was staring at him hard. 'Are you hearing yourself? You've gone way past sensitive; now you're just being pathetic!'

He felt his inner child stomping. 'Well, you know, sometimes it just feels good to roll around in it since I can't do anything to change it!'

'But you *are* doing something to change it. You're *in* a fricking Franc Abdali film! *You* did that, Alden. *You!* You're on your way. And once you've got *Darkness* under your belt the sands *will* shift.' She sighed, and then her tone and gaze softened. 'Come on, Alden. You're better than this…'

He felt his bristles falling flat. She was right. He *was* better than this. How had he even got himself caught in this pointless downward spiral? Ah, yes. The devastating notion that she might be starting to see him the way the world saw him.

He searched her eyes. No sign of it now—if it had ever been there at all. And absolutely no point dwelling on the likely aftermath of their broken 'engagement' when there was the huge, more immediate problem of Franc's last-minute, casually hurled curveball. He felt his stomach tightening. The thought of it was springing locks inside him, but how would it be, in reality? Him. Her. *Together.* And how would he even know how to pitch—

'Hey…' She was leaning in, a smile just visible at the corners of her mouth. 'It'll all work out. You just need to focus, take one step at a time.' And then her smile opened out, dimpling her cheeks. 'I think we sold ourselves to Franc anyway, so that's the first step nailed.'

His heart leapt. *Clever Jules.* She'd just opened a door, saving him from the stomach-churning prospect of looking for one.

'Yes, we did.' He tugged at his bow-tie to loosen it, to let some air in. 'We did such a good job of selling ourselves to Franc that he's invited you to come with me to Cannes…'

* * *

'What?'

He couldn't be serious, surely?

'I said...' His hand fell from his collar. 'You're invited to Cannes. With me.'

Her heart bumped. He *was* being serious. Serious and, also, curiously watchful.

She searched his face. Did he *want* her to go? Was he waiting for her to show some enthusiasm?

Her belly fluttered then shrank. She definitely wasn't feeling that. Faking for one evening had been weird enough. *Confusing.* Holding his hand, liking the feel of it. Kissing his cheek, liking the smoothness of it. Breathing in his lovely smell close to, liking it. And what about those deep looks, that firm hand on her waist, vaguely possessive, and that divine, disconcerting warmth pulsing through the silk of the dress he'd insisted on buying for her?

Insisted...

Because he felt he owed her something in return for the acting. Because all of it was only acting. *Acting!* And going to Cannes with him would mean more of the same, except that it wouldn't be remotely the same, would it? Because now, thanks to her, they were 'engaged', and engaged people generally shared a room. A bed!

Her belly spun.

Just, no!

No, no, no!

And whatever was going on in his head right now, whatever he was trying to hide behind his gaze, she couldn't entertain it. Going to Cannes with him as his fiancée, spending a whole week with people she didn't know—*Natasha*—was absolutely not happening!

She settled back in her seat, massaging her wrist, using the moment to steady herself, then she smiled over. 'Well, that's very kind of Franc, I must say, but I don't want to go.'

Something retreated in his eyes and her heart dipped. *Too blunt.* She should have supplied a reason, *should* supply one. 'I mean, there'd be no point in me coming. You'll be working all the time.'

'I won't be.'

Should have stuck with blunt.

She bit back a sigh. 'How come?'

He put a finger to his eyelid. 'Because Franc's super tired and wants to take some time out whilst he's at home, to recharge etcetera. He mentioned it before you arrived—asked if we would mind having a bit of down time while we're there. Obviously, I had to say I was fine with it, because what else could I say?' He rubbed his eye and then his hand fell back into his lap. 'But, if *you* were there, then it would actually be fine because you're my darling fiancée...'

His gaze was steady, beseeching, putting the squeeze on her heart.

'Alden, please, don't do this.'

His palms went up with only a touch of jazz hands. 'I'm not doing anything! I'm just saying that if you were there then down time would be fun.' He pushed his lips out. 'Tash has been to Franc's place before. She says it's fabulous. Sea views, swimming pool, tennis court...'

As if she was remotely interested in what Natasha thought or said.

She pushed her own lips out. 'I don't play tennis.'

His chin dipped. 'I know you don't, Miss Churlish, but you could give it a go. I could teach you!'

'Oh, well, that clinches it, then. Count me in!'

'Really...?'

'No, Alden!' What was with him that he hadn't even caught her sarcasm? 'Not *really*. Not at all! I can't spend an entire week pretending to be your fiancée. I told you before, I'm not Greta Garbo.'

He produced a short, amazed laugh. 'I disagree. That was quite the performance you put in earlier.'

'Well, it was a once-in-a-lifetime performance, okay? I'm done now.'

His face fell, making her heart squeeze again.

'Why do you even *want* me to go? I mean, you'll have your cast mates. And Franc.'

'Oh yeah, hanging around with Natasha and

a bunch of people I don't know very well, and who don't know me—all of us going through the vague rituals of buddying up.' His fingers drifted to the dashboard, flicking a switch. Up. Down. Up. Down. 'Don't get me wrong, I'm all on board with Franc's methodology, building bonds for the sake of the film, but at the end of the day they're semi-relationships.'

Not like us, he wasn't saying, but it was what he meant; she could tell.

And then he was settling back into his seat, looking over. 'As to why I want you to come...' His lips tightened. 'I've got one selfish reason and one that's completely selfless.'

Her heart gave. Why was he talking about selfish when he didn't have a selfish bone in his body? He was a good person. Just overly sensitive to what others said and thought about him, and because of it he was prone to getting himself tangled up, which could give the impression that he was self-absorbed, but he wasn't. It was more that he was desperate for validation.

His parents' fault, for always holding the family medical tradition over his head like a Sword of Damocles! For never acknowledging his choice, his talent, his achievements.

She did her best to take up the slack, to shore him up, because that was what he'd done for her when Mum split, when everything in her world had been collapsing. If it hadn't been for him, she would never have scraped through her exams, made it through school. And, if it wasn't for him, she would never have picked herself up so quickly after Sam left.

She drew him back into focus. She didn't want to open herself up to being persuaded to go to Cannes, but she couldn't not ask him the question. Couldn't not at least hear him out, because he was her best friend, and that was what friends were for, wasn't it?

'Okay, I'm listening. Tell me your selfish reason.'

He smiled a brief, grateful smile and then he laced his fingers together, flexing and stretching them the way he did when he had a story to tell. 'So…when you went to powder your nose, Joe was telling me he has it on good authority that Hayden Coulter is in talks with Silvermount Films…'

She felt her pulse quickening. Hayden Coulter was the lead actor in *Darkness*, playing Saul. It was the part that Alden had really wanted, but Hayden had been cast ahead of everyone else, so he hadn't had a chance to audition.

'As in now?'

'Yep! Seems there's a strong chance he's going to pull out of *Darkness* because Silvermount wants him to do the *Taurus Trilogy.*'

'Oh, my God!'

The Taurus Trilogy by Raz Rocco was the biggest literary phenomenon since Harry Potter—a dark, intelligent, dystopian epic. It would undoubtedly be the blockbuster movie franchise of the decade.

'OMG indeed!' His eyebrows went up. 'Obviously, it's an awesome opportunity for Hayden, but it's also—'

'An awesome opportunity for *you*, because if he drops out then—'

'The Saul part is up for grabs. Yes! I mean, I don't know who else auditioned for Saul, so maybe there's a close second in the running, but...' His gaze drifted for a beat and then his eyes came back, bright as fever. 'God, Jules, if I could convince Franc to give me a crack at it...'

It would mean the world, make his parents finally sit up and pay attention. It was all there in his eyes, burning hard—the dream part, the chance to play his favourite character in his all-time favourite book.

She bit her lip. 'You need to impress Franc, then—*really* impress him.'

'Which I'll do a whole lot better if you're there with me...' His eyes were reaching in, pleading. 'You'd keep me calm, Jules—steady. You'd talk all the sense into me if I started losing it...'

She felt her heart turning over. He was targeting the softest part of her, the part that always wanted to help him, to be there for him. Targeting her with the most compelling reason imaginable.

The only thing was that, if tonight was anything to go by, going there as his fiancée wouldn't do much for her own sense of calm. Being there as his fiancée would mean more touching, more hand-holding, more confusion…

Her stomach pulsed. Like when they were sixteen and he was coming round all the time to help her revise, talking her through something, eyes flashing blue, making her heart skip and flutter. And those times when he'd been looking down, sketching a diagram, explaining, and she had found herself looking at his mouth, the movements of his lips, wondering…

And there had been other times too, lying together on his bed, watching those films he loved, the ones he wouldn't let her talk through, when his foot had sometimes accidentally caught hers as he shifted and she'd felt the moment stretching, a potent second that had seemed charged with possibility.

But nothing had ever happened. And she was glad—*glad!*—because, if it had, they'd undoubtedly have been history by now, and she wouldn't have had her best friend, her soul mate, a soul mate who was right this second asking her to do something that could row her back into that land of confusion…

Or would it, actually?

For sure, she'd felt some old strings tugging the day he'd come over after Sam left—and, *admit it*, a few new ones too—but that could have just been the tequila effect. Aside from that, she hadn't really thought about him in that way for years.

Maybe she was feeling confused tonight, not so much because of him but because of her own stupid susceptibilities, because she was a sucker for any kind of physical affection, especially when she was lonely, as she was right now, when she didn't have someone.

Probably psychological! Bound up with Mum leaving, Dad shrinking into himself afterwards instead of gathering her in. *Whatever!* She couldn't help the way she was. She needed to feel cherished, loved, craved it so much that, barring a few dry spells, she'd always had someone, always a long-term relationship. Like Sam…

'What am I for, Jules?'

Her heart caught. That damn question, settling into the silence like smoke after he'd gone. It was still there, circling, tormenting her, even though she was over him. Well and truly. But she *did* miss his touch—*being touched*—and tonight Alden had been the one touching her. Holding her hand, her waist, pressing warm lips to her forehead, supplying her with the very thing she missed. No wonder she was all over the place—

'Do you want to hear the selfless reason now?'

Collar loose, tie hanging, smiling into her eyes…

She took a breath. 'Go on then.'

His head tilted. 'You're still free next week, right?'

Because of Sam, he was being careful not to say, but he knew she'd cancelled Santorini, sent Sam his half of the money back. He knew that she hadn't booked in any wedding work that week because, in the throes of her post-Sam heartbreak, she'd told him she was thinking of going away on her own somewhere. Cornwall. The Hebrides. Mars! And because he was her best friend, the person she talked to all the time, he also knew that she'd never got round to booking anything.

She felt a sigh trickling out. 'You know very well I am.'

'Well…' He shifted in his seat a little. 'I'm not saying I'm happy about the reason for that, but it means that you *could* actually come with me, and, if you did, then I could look after you.'

She bit her lip. He was pulling out that comfort blanket, dangling it…

'I *want* to look after you, Jules. You're always looking after me, and you took such a tumble over *you know who*, and…' His gaze was softening, filling with unbearable kindness. 'I don't know, you just work so bloody hard all the time, and you've hurt your wrist, and I think you deserve a break, a bit of sun and funshine!'

A brief smile touched his lips. 'I can give you that if you let me. All you have to do is come. And I *know* it's a big ask, because of the luvvies and the faking, but if we plan things right we can probably dodge the others most of the time, so it'll be okay.' His chin dipped. 'Whatever happens, I'll *make* it okay, I promise, make sure you have a good time. Please, Jules…' And then he was leaning in, giving her nowhere to hide. 'Say yes. Let me make a fuss of you.'

Impossible!

How could she think straight when he was this deep into caring mode, filling her bandwidth, making it all sound so easy? Avoiding the others to minimise the faking. She bit her lip. That would certainly limit the dreaded confusion, leaving just the 'sun and funshine'…

A proper break!

With her best friend in the world.

On the French Riviera…

She felt a tingle, her pulse starting to quicken. She *was* free. And they were bound to have fun. Which she needed. Just a week, after all, and he *did* need her. What harm could there be?

None!

She reconnected with his gaze, feeling a smile starting to fizz. 'For the record, thwacking a ball over a net is *not* my idea of a good time.'

His eyes lit, momentarily incredulous, and then he let out a short, smiling breath. 'Okay. Absolutely no tennis!' One eyebrow went up. 'What about sightseeing? Old churches, narrow cobbled streets, little tucked-away bistros…?'

Where there would be no chance whatsoever of bumping into Natasha. She caught her bottom lip between her teeth to slow down her smile. 'I like that better.'

'Great!' He leaned back and then his finger went up. 'I'll hire a car—something fun. We can do the coast. Saint Tropez!' He was electric-smiling now, making her stomach, her veins, her whole body tingle. 'You can channel your inner Brigitte Bardot and I'll be Alain Delon. Remember him? Won Best Actor in *Notre Histoire*.'

'The really hot guy with the devastating blue eyes?'

'Yep. So I'll be him—perfect casting, obviously—and you can be BB. And we'll sightsee, and eat crêpes, and ogle the big yachts and pretend we're beautiful people… Except, obviously, you won't need to pretend—'

'Alden!'

He blinked. 'Yes.'

'Now I've said I'll go; will you please stop talking and take me home?'

His cheeks creased, and then he was reaching

for the ignition. 'Now you've said yes, my sweet darling, I won't only stop talking. I'll throw in an engagement ring for good measure.'

CHAPTER SIX

ALDEN CRACKED OPEN the velvet box. He hadn't been thinking of Grandmother's emerald-and-diamond engagement ring when he'd promised Jules a ring, but using it seemed appropriate, given that his grandmother had always had a soft spot for Jules.

'When are you going to ask that lovely Juliana out on a proper date?'

He felt a smile coming, felt his hand going to his face instinctively. He'd used to blush, turn away and busy himself with something to hide his flaming cheeks, but those bright, knowing eyes saw everything.

Grandmother knew he had a serious crush on Jules, that he couldn't wait to go over to her place in the evenings to help her with her maths and science. At sixteen, there'd been nothing better in the world than the way Jules looked at him, that soft glow of admiration in her eyes because he got the things that she didn't: quadratic equations; enzymes; electrons. He loved seeing that happy spark jumping when she started to understand, loved that he was able to put back something good after all the pain she'd had over Paulina walking out.

But mostly he loved it because it felt like giving back. Giving back for smiling that first day; for noticing him; for giving him the time of day. For listening to him with that supportive gleam in her eyes while he offloaded to her about the expectations his parents had that he would follow them into medicine like his brother and sister.

The sacred Phillips family tradition! Doctors for three generations and let no one forget it! All that weight pressing down on him, crushing a heart that wanted—*yearned*—for something else.

He couldn't talk to his parents or his teachers about acting. They all had him pegged as a 'bright boy' destined for 'great things', none of which they saw taking place on stage or screen. And he hadn't wanted to fight about it.

Instead, he'd contented himself with doing the school shows, going to the drama club, hoping they might twig, take the hint. But somehow his parents decided he was simply 'having fun', and his teachers just praised him for rounding himself out so nicely.

Only Jules knew what was really going on inside him. Only Jules understood. And, because she was the only one he could talk to, because she got him so thoroughly, no matter how hard she made his heart flip and tumble—no matter much he longed to kiss her—he hadn't wanted to risk losing her precious friendship by trying it.

Not that he hadn't used to think about it all the time, hadn't sometimes ventured…

Lying side by side on his bed watching movies, pillows tucked, elbows propped, curtains drawn for the full cinematic experience, he might nudge her foot *by accident*, holding his breath, strung so tight he could have snapped, holding on, and on, wondering if she would respond, nudge him back, *start* something… But she never did.

And it was fine, he'd rationalised. For the best. Because they were friends and that was worth more. And anyway, she was going through so much at home. Let down by her mum, and by a dad who didn't seem able to step into the breach. The last thing Jules needed was him screwing things up between them, letting her down too, causing her more pain.

Because he was bound to, being clueless and everything. She was gorgeous. Perfect! And he was just an infatuated, shorter-than-average, hormone-addled brainbox, with a passion for theatre, and hair that would never behave.

So, he'd tucked his crush away, turned his attention to other girls, but the number of rejections he'd got soon confirmed what he'd always suspected: he was *not* a catch. Jules was, though. And, once they got to sixth form, she was being caught constantly, mostly by tall, good-looking boys who played rugby.

He'd felt the odd jealous twinge back then, but he'd got past it, grown up. Figuratively. *Literally.* By the time he started medical school, he was four inches taller and quite the dab hand with at least two different types of hair product. Suddenly girls seemed interested, and he'd lapped it up, because female interest considerably softened the blow of having to study medicine.

As for Jules… He didn't regret a thing. Far from it. Not sacrificing their friendship on the altar of a blundering teenage romance was the best decision he'd ever made, because all these years later he still had her, didn't he? Friend. Soul mate. Saviour. And now…he drew the ring back into focus…fiancée.

Fake fiancée.

A sharp ache caught him across the forehead, triggering a twitch at the corner of his eye.

Why had he worked on her to go when straight off she'd been unequivocal about not wanting to? He could have messaged Franc to say that Jules had other plans and couldn't make it. But instead he'd pushed, cajoled, stumbling through a confusion of needs, wants, and desires, all of them selfish!

He snapped the box shut, slid it into his pocket, then pressed a finger to his eyelid, holding it there as he crossed over to the bed and sank down.

It must be a selfish twitch. He never used to be selfish, but now he was. Wanting, needing, *asking* Jules to prop him up, even though she wasn't going to be happy being there with those people. Asking her to fake a relationship with him when, in her own words, she wasn't Greta Garbo.

Granted, she could turn in a convincing performance under duress. Hadn't she knocked the breath clean out of him with that deep look, that hand to his face which had set fire to his blood before Natasha had arrived, dowsing him back to clarity?

God, she was good, performing for Natasha's benefit, meeting the brief he'd given her to be his adoring girlfriend for the night. And it was to protect him from Natasha and make him look settled that she'd gone over and above, announcing that they were engaged.

That was Jules—holding his interests to her heart as if they were her own; celebrating his wins, commiserating when he failed. Wanting for him what he wanted for himself. Wanting his dreams to come true, giving her all for his sake.

He rubbed his eye then fell backwards, staring at the ceiling. Maybe that was why, in the hotel car park, Franc's invitation had suddenly transformed into a bright, wonderful opportunity…

Under normal circumstances, asking Jules to go away with him so he could repay her a little for her friendship and support would have felt weird, because it wasn't their pattern. Their pattern was hanging out when he wasn't on set, or away on location. When she wasn't tied up with work, or with a boyfriend. They liked walking in Hyde Park; taking hours to eat pasta at Luigi's in Covent Garden; checking out the vintage fashion at Portobello market, losing themselves in the crowd, blending in so that he was hardly ever recognised.

Their pattern was home turf and old haunts. But, thinking about Cannes, he'd started picturing all the ways he could spoil her. He'd pictured her laughing, burying her toes into soft, white sand, hair blowing, eyes shining. Happy! Because of him…

His heart bucked. Was that why he'd pushed her to go—for himself, so that he could see himself reflected in her warm gaze and feel good? Not just good, but… Oh, God! Was he sliding backwards into his crush days? The blood-tingling days of movies and cinematic bedroom gloom, his tentative, nudging foot and that eternal charged moment that followed?

He rolled himself up, inhaling hard. No, no, no. *No!*

He was *not* doing this for himself.

He was *not* hoping for anything for himself.

He was *not* regressing…

He was…*panicking!*

He glanced at the bulging holdall he'd set by

the door and instantly his stomach was roiling again.

Panic—that must be it. He was jittering because it was D-day—departure day, almost departure moment—and because what they were trying to pull off was…

His heart bounced. *Ludicrous!* This whole scenario was ridiculous: having to fake an engagement; having to share a room like an engaged couple! How was he even in this position? Because of the part, and because of the other part he really wanted, and because Franc had been concerned about Natasha and him. And now Natasha wanted sex…and Jules had leapt in and now…

Jules… And probably it was the prospect of all the touching that was throwing him backwards, because usually they didn't. And now they would have to—at least a bit, when they were with the others. And what he couldn't get out of his mind, couldn't stop feeling, was her tender thumb tracking over his cheekbone at the party; that intensity in her eyes, the way he'd lost his breath and all the blood rushing to…and maybe this whole thing was a very, *very* bad idea.

Enough!

He inhaled hard to steady himself then got to his feet.

Undoubtedly it *was* a very bad idea, but it was done now and there was a lot riding on it, so he had to get a grip. Jules was his best friend, and he wasn't going to jeopardise that friendship by letting a bit of hand-holding stir up old desires that no longer had any currency.

He patted his pocket for the ring box, then went for his bag. Not much he could do about his body. Jules was lovely, and when she touched him his blood sprang to life, but that was a man thing, wasn't it? Men were pitiful creatures, and he was more pitiful than most. The main thing was, he knew it, and that had to count for something.

CHAPTER SEVEN

FRANC OPENED THE double doors and stood aside. 'Here you are…'

She felt her nerves jolt, even though she was braced for this, even though she and Alden had comprehensively strategised the business of sharing a room.

It had been their 'driving to the airport' conversation—at least it had been once they'd got past the engagement-ring conversation. His grandmother's ring! Bequeathed to him because, when he was little, he liked to count the diamonds that circled the glowing emerald, used to like hearing the story of how his grandfather had journeyed all the way to the Emerald City to find it.

A lovely concoction.

A stunning ring.

The last ring she'd expected him to produce, because this one had provenance, was meant to be for his real fiancée when that day came. But he'd waved away her objections. He'd said that his grandmother had always liked her, so absolutely wouldn't have minded her wearing it. The fact that it was a perfect fit, he said, could only be a signal from 'the other side' that his grandmother approved.

She wasn't so sure that Grandmother Phillips would remotely approve of the charade they were playing, and she was frankly terrified of losing the precious ring, although since it fitted her finger well—nice and snug—she was probably worrying unnecessarily. The point of it was to work, and it did. It was going to do a fine job of fooling everyone.

Meanwhile, she wasn't doing a very good job of fooling anyone, was she, standing here with warmth creeping into her cheeks and an advancing, thundering awareness that what she was looking at was *their* designated space, the space they were going to be sharing for a whole week...

They'd squared it away piece by piece: how Alden would kip on the sofa if there was one, or on the floor if there wasn't, and how she would have the bed. But she wasn't seeing a sofa, just a light, spacious room with a polished, dark-wood floor and a *huge* bed, stretching like the Sahara, except it was a white Sahara, all crisp cotton and plump, inviting pillows, which she really needed to stop staring at now, otherwise Franc might think that she'd never seen a bed before.

She took a little breath. 'It's a gorgeous room, Franc. Really lovely.'

He gestured inside, smiling. 'You *can* go in, you know…'

Instead of standing, rooted to the spot, he was obviously thinking.

She felt Alden's propelling hand between her shoulder blades and planted her feet, resisting. She couldn't have Franc thinking she was weird, or reluctant. She needed to manufacture something credible out of her hesitation.

She smiled back. 'I was just savouring it for a moment, taking it all in.' She paused another moment for effect, then stepped forward, heading for the windows, hoping to exude poise and confidence. 'I love these high windows…' And then suddenly a thrill caught her in the chest, stripping the poise clean away. 'Look, Alden! There's a balcony!'

He came to stand beside her, glancing into her eyes, his own radiating amusement. 'So there is.'

'All the south-facing rooms have canopied balconies—for shade, you understand.' Franc was busy with the French doors, unlatching them, spreading them wide, letting in a breath of breeze that smelt of the not-too-distant sea.

'Come…' He went ahead, beckoning them out, needlessly straightening the two wicker chairs that flanked a low table. 'This is a very nice place to sit with a book and a glass of wine.'

Was he for real, talking about reading when the view was as glorious as this? Bright blue sky, bright blue sea, green slopes to the left and right of them, dotted with the occasional terracotta roof.

Alden was already at the balustrade, leaning over. 'I think I'd find it hard to sit and read when there's all this to look at...'

She held in a smile. On the same page, as always.

'Well, of course, reading is *not* obligatory...' Franc was chuckling, and then his finger went up. 'Except when it comes to the script.'

'I know the script already!' Alden smiled, imparting exactly the right amount of casual confidence with no sign of that usual pesky shirt tail.

'Ah, yes, I remember.' Franc's head tilted, expressing interest. '*The Darkness of Shadows* is your favourite book, isn't it?'

Alden grinned. 'Only of *all time*. I was fourteen the first time I read it. Blew me away! I felt such a connection with it...'

Because of the Saul character, caught between duty to his family and the yearnings of his own heart—like *him*. She'd heard it a thousand times.

She let her eyes go past him to the view, but after a few moments she realised that she was looking at his rear, at the way it was shifting inside his jeans as he talked and gesticulated.

She pressed a finger to her lip. Such a neat rear. So tight. So firm. She felt a little nest of heat building, a guilty tug low down inside, but she couldn't make herself look away. Alden's tush was too sublime. Scrumptious.

Scrumptious?

Wasn't that the word Natasha had used in the same breath as 'horny'? Oh, God, and now it was stuck in her brain, jammed in hard, playing on repeat: *scrumptious, scrumptious, scrumptious...* And 'horny' was chiming in too: *horny, horny, horny...* And how could she even be thinking these things? Hadn't she'd promised herself not to cross any wires, not to let any confusion start? Alden was her friend, and his friendship was everything, so she needed to look away now— *unthink* these thoughts—because thinking about him like this was wrong, plain wro—

'Isn't that right, Jules?'

She jumped, found Alden looking back at her over his shoulder with quizzical eyes.

Was he onto her? Had he noticed her checking him out? Her heart thumped. If they'd been in London, she could have waltzed around it with a joke, turned it into a tease, but she couldn't do that with Franc here.

Or…maybe she could. Subtly. Make light of it and sweep it away as if it were nothing. Which it was, of course. *Nothing!* A brief mental dalliance borne of sunshine and blue sky and Alden's un-deniably scrumptious denim-clad tush thrust out so that even a nun would have been hard pressed not to feel a quiver.

'Sorry. I was lost in the view—must have tuned out…' She waited for the admission to register in his eyes and then she smiled. 'What were you asking me?'

His gaze held hers for half a beat and then he straightened, turned, pointedly parking his rear against the balustrade. 'I was just saying to Franc that I've read *Darkness* so many times that I know every line in it….' His eyes widened into hers. 'Every word the characters say…'

Her heart pulsed. So he was already going for it, laying a keystone for when—*if*—Hayden dropped out, calling on her to be a witness. And what had she been doing? Ogling, courting inner confusion instead of paying attention…

She swallowed, nodding to signal that she was on it, then she looked at Franc, rolling her eyes to seem like a long-suffering fiancée.

'Oh, yes, indeed.' She shook her head for good measure. 'You should see his copy, Franc. Not being funny but it's a *shadow* of its former self.'

Franc chuckled.

She pushed on. 'And he's not exaggerating. I think he could actually recite the whole book verbatim.'

'I could probably have a pretty good stab at it myself after writing the screenplay.' Franc's eyebrows flickered. 'Not the easiest story to adapt.' And then his gaze settled on Alden. 'I shall be looking to you for some input if the read-through throws up anything.'

Alden's face lit. 'You got it.'

'Good.' Franc pressed his palms together and then he was moving towards the doors. 'Now, I'll leave you to get settled. Come down when you're ready. I think everyone's here now, so we can get the introductions out of the way, start getting to know one another.'

Alden shut the doors after Franc then stood, holding onto the handles, trying to steady himself.

Why was he freaking out all of a sudden? It wasn't as if he'd never been alone in a room with Jules before. They were alone in rooms all the time—her work room, for example, and her sitting room. *His* sitting room. Sometimes they were the only ones left in a restaurant. So, this wasn't unusual. This aloneness was no different from any other.

His heart clopped.

Except that they were 'engaged'. Sharing a bedroom in Franc Abdali's home. In Cannes. In France. And Jules had just been staring at his bum; she'd admitted as much. What was he supposed to make of that? Of her…?

Another hefty clop.

Is she staring at it now?

He spun himself round, right into the bright beam of her breaking smile.

'So that seemed to go well…'

She was sitting at the end of the bed, looking chic in her white sleeveless shirt and slender, red cropped pants, her hair wound up and stabbed through, not with her usual pencil but with some tortoiseshell contraption because: *'I thought I'd better up my game now that we're betrothed.'*

Upping her game… Meanwhile he'd put on his battered Levi's and a random tee-shirt to blend in, so he wouldn't be recognised at the airport.

He felt a tingle. Was that it…? Could it be that, after the engagement-ring conversation, and the sensible talk they'd had about how they were going to manage sharing the room; and after all the hoo-hah of collecting the bright yellow rental convertible—*'Oh, Alden. It's sooo sweet!'*—and the mind-bending challenge of programming the incomprehensible sat nav so they could risk life and limb on a million lethal twisty roads simply to get here, outside on the balcony she had finally registered his uber-casual attire and not much liked it? Could it be that when she'd said she was lost in the view she was being sarcastic?

Yes… *Yes!*

He felt his spirit settling. That fitted. Jules was good at sarcasm. Even her eyebrows were sarcastic. Except for now. Right now they were sliding up, waiting for him to reply. About it seeming to go well. With Franc.

He ran a hand over his face. 'I hope so. I wasn't

sure about leaping in with all that "knowing the
script" business, but then I thought, why waste
the opportunity?'

'Well, you definitely didn't do that, and good
for you, because look where it got you!' Her lips
curved up sweetly. 'You're now Franc's official
script supervisor!' And then her smile faded a
little. 'I'm sorry I fell behind.'

Was she trying to be funny, using the word
'behind'? He felt a smile rising, a tease taking
shape.

'It's okay. Getting lost in the view is understandable.' He slid his hands into his back pockets, rocking on his heels a bit. 'I realise I'm looking rather
irresistible today…'

Her cheeks pinked. 'Oh, is that right?' And
then her gaze was sharpening into his, glinting
mischief. 'You must be so pleased we've got a
room with double doors. Imagine how awful it
would be if you were to get trapped in here with
your great big head.'

He felt a chuckle vibrating. This was home
turf, and on home turf he never missed a cue.

'Ouch…' He snapped himself in half, clutching at his belly, contorting his face, moaning,
and swaying, staggering towards her until she
was giggling, scrambling backwards on the bed,
kicking her feet.

'Stop!' Laughing into his eyes. 'I hurt you, I get
it. I'm sorry.'

But he didn't want to stop, because making Jules laugh was everything. It felt good. Normal. And he wanted this, this warm feeling of being friends, laughing together. This was what he needed to hold onto—the feeling he needed to remember if anything weird started throwing him off, poking ancient fires back to life.

He took hold of her ankles, leaning in to make the light spark in her eyes. 'Exactly how sorry are you…?'

She stilled, panting a little, holding his gaze with a slight frown, and then her expression was softening, opening out, and suddenly all the breath in his lungs was gone. He noticed her ankles in his hands, the smooth warmth of her skin, the hard bone.

His heart jerked. What was he doing, touching her like this? They didn't do this. They weren't… And now what…? If he dropped her like a hot coal it would only highlight the weirdness, but not letting go meant he was stranded here, dry-mouthed and pulsing, and she was just looking at him, looking and looking, except… His heart jerked again. Except now something was surfacing in her eyes, something that looked like bemusement, and a smile was growing on her lips, one of her wicked ones, which could only mean—*thank God*—that she was about to shake him free with a come-back.

'Actually, I take that back. I'm not sorry at

all.' Her voice clipped him, and then suddenly she was moving, shifting, making it easy for him to take his hands back and stand clear while she wriggled herself free, flouncing off the bed.

He felt a ripple of gratitude. This was Jules all over, always making things easy for him.

'Truth is, you're nowhere near irresistible.' She was folding her arms now, looking him up and down. 'I mean, seriously—*those* jeans?'

He looked down to examine the rips and frays, trying to think of something to say, but he didn't have a clever come-back, just a bleak, impending sense of impasse.

She didn't care about his jeans. She was only mopping up the mess he'd made, setting them upright again, trying to make things normal. Trouble was, nothing about this was normal. *Him* especially. He seemed to be bouncing from one extreme to another, full of fear one moment, too bold the next, too full-on. If he wasn't careful, he was going to wreck everything and then Jules wouldn't have the nice holiday he'd promised her, *wanted* to give her.

He needed to fix this, drag himself out into the open before he lost his mind, and his friend.

He steadied himself with a breath then lifted his gaze to hers. 'I don't think I can do this banter, Jules…'

'Okay…?'

Which was her way of saying: *talk to me. Let it all out.*

Not a problem. He could talk for England, but making sense was another thing. On the other hand, she was adept at sifting through his nonsense, so maybe he just needed to let himself go.

'I feel strange. All over the place...' *Touching you...* 'And I'm sorry for that thing I did, grabbing your ankles.' He licked his lips. 'I didn't mean to. I think I'm tense, so I'm trying too hard to be normal and ending up being the opposite...'

Her eyes held him for a second and then she was unfolding her arms, sighing. 'We're both tense. See how I stalled at the door when Franc was showing us in?'

'Yeah, but you recovered well, whereas I'm...' He rubbed at a knot of tension in his neck, felt relief loosening his tongue. 'I'm trying to pretend I'm fine—and I'm not saying I'm not basically fine, or that I won't be soon—but the truth is, right now, I'm feeling weird. Are you feeling weird?'

Something unlocked in her gaze. 'Very.' And then she was going back to the bed, plonking herself down. 'But we're bound to. I mean, we're doing this extraordinary thing, and we're in this strange place.' Her eyes came to his. 'And I know we've talked about sharing the room, but even so...'

'Exactly.' His heart thumped. 'Now that we're here...'

He let his words run out, letting his eyes slide around the room past the small desk in the corner with the quaint angular chair, past the fitted wardrobes and the slightly ajar door that hinted at the *en suite* beyond, looking for a sofa, a *chaise longue*, anything upholstered.

Her voice broke in. 'There isn't a sofa.'

'Maybe there's a *chaise* or something in the bathroom…' He went to push the door open.

'Oh!' Somehow Jules was right beside him. 'It's a wet room!'

All sleek, shiny marble and gleaming chrome, two sinks with a wide mirror over, and, through the window, a sea view to die for, but no *chaise*, no seating of any kind. No sofa. No comfy armchair. No outdoor seating unit with deep, removable cushions that he could use to take the sting out of the hard floor. Nowhere feasible for him to sleep.

His throat went tight. He wouldn't—*couldn't*—suggest sharing the bed, not after that ankle-grabbing stunt he'd just pulled. Suggesting it would only put Jules in an awkward position, and there'd been more than enough awkwardness already. They were both feeling weird. He didn't want to make things worse.

Besides, it was only a week.

He took a backwards step, shot her what he hoped was a determined smile. 'It's okay. I'll tell

Franc I feel the cold, ask him for an extra duvet. I'll lay it down, sleep on that.'

'You'll do no such thing!' She was shaking her head at him. 'First, you're wearing jeans that seem to be held together with holes, so telling Franc you feel the cold isn't going to wash. Second, a duvet isn't going to soften the floor at all. Third, you've got to be fresh and firing on all cylinders this week, because if you're not then this whole charade will have been for nothing.'

Her eyes flicked to the bed then came back, fully loaded.

'And fourth, do you honestly think I could sleep a single wink in that great big comfy bed, knowing that you were lying awake, uncomfortable, on the floor?'

His heart gave. Only Jules could slay him like this, humble him so utterly. He wanted to put his arms around her and pull her close, kiss her hair, but he couldn't. It would shoot them right back to Weird Central, and he didn't want to go there again.

He let his gaze open into hers. 'No.'

'Okay, then. We'll share the bed.' And then her lips were quirking into a wicked little smile. 'That said, if you snore, I reserve the right to banish you to the balcony.'

CHAPTER EIGHT

'AFTER YOU, DARLING…' Alden was holding the door, twinkling, looking fresh after his shower, nice in his soft shirt and combats.

Handsome!

Her stomach dipped. Why couldn't she seem to switch off her antenna, the one that was constantly picking up the light in his eyes, the sweet shape of his mouth, the drape of his shirt, that delectable tush? The whole time they'd been unpacking, she'd felt awareness tingling, vibrating inside.

It was like being sixteen again, getting lost in the way his lips moved while his focus was on the page, in the way his hair curled at his nape. Stealing glances. Little ripples dancing through. Except she'd been innocent then. Her imagination had only stretched as far as his warm mouth, the sweet taste of his tongue, the soft spring of his hair. Now her imagination was deep-diving.

So wrong!

Maybe it was proximity. She wasn't used to

spending this much time with him all at once, wasn't used to talking about feelings that were *theirs*, borne of a situation that belonged to *them*, that they had to deal with together. Much easier propping him up when he was falling apart over some woman, falling against him when she was sad over some guy. But now they were having to navigate the weirdness of being together in this crazy situation, sharing a room—a bed!

And yes, talking about it, sharing their feelings about the weirdness, settling the sleeping arrangement like two sensible friends, had cleared the air in a way, but it had also deepened the sense of closeness, woven in a new confusing thread of intimacy. Or it had for her, anyway.

And now she could feel two threads tugging— the friendship one and other one as well. Because he was looking heavenly, smelling heavenly, holding out his arm for her to come with that warm, fake-fiancé crinkle in his eyes that was almost too convincing.

And maybe *that* was the part of the problem— how good an actor he was. But she *had* to stop getting herself all confused, letting that other thread tangle and twist, because this was her friend standing in the doorway, *not* her love interest. And she needed him always to be her friend, needed him never to change or disappear, like Mum had.

If she carried on like this, allowing herself to

get hung up on him, he was going to notice and then, because he was Alden, he would start dissecting it, getting all angsty about it—probably— and then everything *would* change between them and she might lose him, and, if that happened, God help her, she would never find her way back.

Time to rein in, pick up her cue and focus on the excruciating hours ahead. Mingling! Sitting around the table eating dinner with strangers— *Natasha!*—supporting Alden in every possible way so that Franc would see him in the round, as the one and only contender for Saul. This was her mission and she needed to get on with it.

She drew up a smile and walked towards him, batting her eyelashes, slipping into fake-fiancée mode. 'You're such a gentleman, babe.'

'I try.' She felt his hand connecting briefly with her back as she stepped into the hallway, and then he was turning to close the doors. 'By the way, I like it when you call me "babe".'

Her heart misfired. Was this her fake fiancé talking or her friend?

'What I mean is that it feels right for us.' He turned back, smiling. 'If you could throw in the odd "babe" in front of the others, that would be good.'

His eyes were merry, glinting with mischief, but still, it felt like a weird conversation to be having. She'd called him "babe" that one time at the party to push the point in front of Natasha, but usually she wouldn't use it precisely because it sounded so contrived. Still, if it was what he wanted…

She swallowed. 'Okay.'

He tilted his head. 'Any special requests yourself?'

'No!' *More weirdness.* 'I mean, just Jules is fine.'

His eyebrows lifted. 'You're not into any little pet names or anything?'

She flicked a glance along the hall to catch her breath. What was he doing, other than making the floor beat under her feet? She didn't favour any pet names, and anyway, this was hardly the moment to be—

'God, I wish you could see your face.'

And then suddenly his features contracted, and he was laughing, throwing his head back, helpless with it.

She felt relief crashing in, a smile breaking loose. He was messing with her. *Of course.* Teasing. Because that was what he did—what *they* did all the time when they were being themselves, when they weren't standing in a strange hallway in the south of France with late-afternoon sunshine slanting up the walls. This was normal. And for some reason she hadn't spotted it.

'Poor Jules…' He was wiping his eyes now, shaking his head. 'You're so tense.'

Reading her as always, but was he reading

her correctly? Could he see that he was the one causing the chaos?

She searched his gaze. Open. Warm. Affectionate. But no, he didn't seem to be joining those particular dots, thank God. Which meant she could throw up a diversion…

She put a hand to her shoulder, rubbing it for effect. 'So you thought it would be fun to make it worse?'

'I was trying to lighten you up!' And then his eyebrows dampened. 'Seriously, though, are you okay? You seem distracted.'

'I wonder why?' She stretched her lips into a comedy grimace. 'Oh, yes. It must be the joyful prospect of what's in store downstairs.'

'It'll be fine.' He gave a little shrug. 'We're primed. We've got our backstory.'

On the balcony, strategising, deciding that their own history would be easiest, minus the falling in love and getting engaged part, of course, because their own story gave them lots to draw on, assuming anyone even asked them about their origins…

'Would you feel better holding my hand?' His face slipped back into focus, then his outstretched hand. He smiled. 'I'll do my best to be manly and protective.'

As if he wasn't anyway. But holding his hand would only make things worse, because at the party she'd liked the feel of it, hadn't she? Liked the warmth of it, that lovely sense of connection, and she couldn't let herself get caught up in those feelings again because there was a whole week ahead of them. Of togetherness. Bed-sharing. And barely eight hours in she was already spinning out.

She shook her head. 'Maybe downstairs, if I'm floundering...'

'Right.' He seemed to falter, and then his hand fell back to his side.

She felt a pang. Was he offended? She couldn't live with that.

'What I mean is that I'm supposed to be the one propping *you* up, not the other way around. You need to be doing your thing, concentrating on Franc, being impressive. I'm not exactly relishing tonight, but I'm okay.' She felt a surge of battle strength. 'I definitely don't want you worrying about me.'

'But I do.' His gaze tightened on hers, and then it was softening. 'You should know by now that it's my default setting...'

And just like that her strength was leaving again. Same warm, deep glow in his eyes as on the bed earlier—his hands, her ankles—that feeling that maybe he wanted to, that at any second he might...

But, of course, he hadn't been thinking anything of the kind because he'd apologised, hadn't he? Explained? Said that he was all over the place, trying so hard to be normal that he was overshooting, overdoing everything…

At the airport, overdoing attentiveness—queuing again to get her hot milk for her coffee after they'd given her cold, even though she'd said over and over again that it didn't matter. Overdoing indulgence, renting the 'fun' convertible so he could take her along the coast—yellow because yellow was her favourite colour and not, as he'd claimed, because it was all they'd had left!

Not his fault that he was playing to all of her weaknesses: her craving for care, and comfort, and safety; for that feeling that she was important to someone, worried about by someone. The sweet indulgence was the cherry on top—that, and his electric smile, and the way his shoulders filled that shirt…

She swallowed hard. And now he was overdoing the concern because she was tense and he wanted to wipe it away. But that deep gaze of his was tangling those two threads up again and she couldn't, *couldn't*, afford to unsettle him by letting him see; couldn't risk rocking their boat for the sake of a stupid temporary twisted thread.

She had to break free, shake them out of this moment. She drew in a breath and smiled, going for a tease. 'You might try a system reboot?'

His gaze stilled into hers then cleared. 'You think?' And then he was looking away down the hall. 'We should probably make a move before they send out a search party.'

Her heart crimped. She'd hurt him. *Oh, God!* Why was this so hard? All she was trying to do was to keep herself on the right side of confusion, not spoil things between them, and now it seemed she was doing exactly that!

'Alden…?' His gaze swung back. 'I like that you care about me; I really do. I just don't want you taking your eye off the ball because of me. I'm fine. So just hit that refresh key, okay? Put yourself centre.'

His eyes clouded. 'You don't think I put myself centre more than enough already?' He was shaking his head, admonishing himself. 'I mean, you didn't even want to come, and I—'

'You *didn't* persuade me against my will, Alden.'

He frowned. 'But I—'

'*Persuaded* me with a promise of fun and sunshine, which I fully intend to hold you to.'

A smile ghosted over his features. 'So you're not—'

'Nope! Not regretting it, not one little bit.' And, even if she were, she wouldn't be choosing this particular moment to tell him so.

His brows drew in, puzzling. 'How can you even—?'

'Because I can read your mind.'

He let out a chuckle, clouds all gone. 'Okay, clever clogs. What am I thinking now?'

She felt a wave of relief ebbing through. Twinkling eyes, smile hanging on his lips. Downward spiral averted. They were back in the safe zone, back to being them. She could allow herself a little preening moment.

'You're thinking how awesome I am…'

He pressed a hand to his chest. 'Obviously!'

'Also, you're thinking that we should get going because otherwise they'll be sending out a search party.'

'I said that already.'

'I know. But you're thinking it again now, aren't you?'

For a beat his eyes held her, and then he was laughing, raising his palm, inviting her to a high-five. 'You got me!'

CHAPTER NINE

HE RELEASED A BREATH, slow-counting to ten, trying to relax, but it was no good. How could he relax when Jules was lying just an arm's length or two away, wafting perfume into the air every time she moved? He could feel her body heat filtering over to his side, or maybe he was imagining it.

Whatever! The feeling and the imagining were having an effect on his pulse, making it beat harder and hotter in some places than in others. And the intimate darkness wasn't helping. Neither was the soft, sweet sound of her breathing and the cloaking silence beyond it, a quiet that seemed loaded somehow; that was invoking their long-ago movie afternoons, all that raging awareness and pounding teenage angst, and now there was a throb starting to bounce between his temples and there was only one way to stop it.

He turned his head on the pillow. 'Can we talk?'

The covers shifted, rustling then flapping.
'What about? I mean, we already did the debrief.'

How it had gone downstairs, she meant. Well
enough, they'd agreed. They'd carried off their
charade with zero hiccups, although Jules had
seemed a bit put out when Natasha had asked
him if his parents were still raining on his parade. His stomach tightened. And he hadn't liked
how long she'd spent talking to Hayden, smiling
her lovely smile at him.

Not that he was going to bring either of those
things up. The point was to relieve the tension,
not stir it up.

Jules had been feeling tense enough earlier
before they'd even gone downstairs. Which was
weird, because he'd thought that the big talk
they'd had after Franc left had cleared the air.
He'd thought they were back in their regular
groove, as far as they could be in the circumstances, but then she'd seemed to keep disappearing off into her own head. And she hadn't
twigged the pet names wind-up.

And then it had come out that she was anxious about the evening, so he'd offered to hold
her hand, but she'd turned him down, which had
made him feel stupidly stung. She'd noticed, of
course, and then everything had got muddled
up. And he'd heard himself saying that worrying about her was his default setting. Then there
had been another of those charged, eternal mo-

ments, like on the bed, and she'd said that thing about how he needed to reboot, which he did, because they'd barely been here twelve hours and he was already sliding down the same old walls, feeling the same old longings, which was why he couldn't sleep and…

Oh, God! And now he was so busy running around inside his own head that he was forgetting to answer her question!

Breathe, Alden!

'I didn't have a specific subject in mind.' He turned onto his side because even though he couldn't see her, it felt better to be facing her. 'I just want to talk for a bit, if it's okay with you…'

'Because you're feeling weird?'

Weird, anxious, turned on, terrified…

'How did you guess?'

There was a shuffling noise, a dipping movement in the mattress, and then the outline of her hair came into focus, rim-lit by the thin light bleeding through the shutters. She was facing him now too. 'Because I'm feeling a bit weird as well so, you know, it figured.'

He felt a smile coming, his spirits lifting. They were the same.

'Silly, though, really, isn't it? Feeling weird.'

'Why?'

'Well, what we're feeling weird about is that we're in this bed together, right?'

A small silence swelled. 'It's one of the things, for sure…'

One?

He bit down on his lip. No. She was right. There was almost too much weirdness to quantify.

'Where I'm going with this is—'

'I know where you're going with it. You're thinking about our movie afternoons, aren't you?'

She really *was* a mind reader!

'Yes.'

She sighed. 'That was different, though.'

'Not that different.'

Same awareness; same jittering nerves…

'Excuse me!' She made an indignant little noise. 'We were fully dressed, *on top of* the bed, watching a film that we weren't allowed to talk through. And now we're undressed, in the bed, not watching a film—and you want to talk!'

He pictured her pyjamas: stripy, somewhat voluminous, somewhat fetching.

'You're hardly undressed.'

There was a brief, stunned silence.

'Well, what did you expect me to wear? A pair of boxers and nothing else, like you?'

The image snagged for long, tantalising second.

'I didn't give it a thought.'

Which wasn't true, but he could hardly tell her that more than once he'd caught himself on the road to a fantasy of silk, and narrow straps, her hair tumbling down, before guilt had scythed in and slashed the fantasy to ribbons.

'So, just like your own outfit, then...' Sarcasm on her voice. 'That's if boxers can even be deemed an *outfit* as such!'

He felt mischief sparking. 'It's more of an outfit than I usually wear.'

'And *that* is more than enough information, thank you very much.'

And then she was giggling, making the bed covers jiggle, making a happy little wave slosh over him. This was so much better than buttoning up all rigid and quiet.

He smiled over, even though she probably couldn't see. 'This reminds me of our phone calls...'

'You mean the ones you make when you've just finished a shoot in LA that wake me up because it's the middle of night in London...?'

He winced, but only a bit, because her voice was smiling.

She went on. 'I don't see any similarity. I mean, we don't routinely discuss nightwear.'

'But we have a laugh, don't we? Like now. That's what I was thinking.'

Her voice dipped. 'Yeah.'

He let his eyes close. Such a sweet sound, that soft, smiling whisper of hers. Warm, intimate...

And then suddenly a queasy wave shifted in

his stomach. He'd never thought much of Sam, never thought *about* him as a person with a heart and a mind. He'd never given a thought to how Sam might have felt about Jules slipping out of bed to talk to *him* in the middle of the night.

His belly clenched. *He* wouldn't have liked it if Jules had been his. He'd have been antsy. *Jealous!* Christ, he was only a *fake* fiancé, and yet he'd felt every single one of his bristles standing up, watching her with Hayden.

He dug his fingers into his forehead.

Sam. Sam. Sam.

How had Sam felt? What had Sam thought? About anything?

He drew a blank. *Weird.* Why was he only noticing now that Jules had never really talked to him about Sam? Come to think of it, she'd never really talked about any of the guys she went out with, except to say she'd met them, or that it was over. They seemed to arrive in her life, stay for ever, then depart. And she would cry, and he'd go to mop her up, but she never discussed the ins and outs, listed flaws, failings.

Not like him. He was the post-mortem type, wasn't he? Forensic! Because every fail held a lesson in its hands, something to take forward. But Jules…

Maybe it was because of her mum. When Paulina left, she'd been full of hows and whys, but since then it was as if she'd disconnected that part of herself—decided she wasn't going to put herself through that mill. Logical, if putting yourself through the mill wouldn't change anything or take away the pain.

Still, she'd seemed rather struck on Sam, and Sam had left. For all he knew, his thoughtless nocturnal calls might have been a factor. And now that the thought was in his head, it was going to drive him mad if he didn't say something.

'Jules?'

'Yeah?'

'Can I ask you something?'

'Yeah…'

'Did Sam mind me calling at night?'

Silence.

He felt his stomach tightening, anxiety jumping. Jules was the come-back queen. And she wasn't coming back at him nearly fast enough.

He swallowed hard. 'Jules…?'

And then the covers were tugging and shuffling, and she was on her back, the faint light revealing her profile, the sweet jut of her chin.

'I don't know…' She sounded as if the thought was new to her, perplexing. 'He didn't say anything.'

He felt a jolt of relief and then a small, unexpected flick of anger. 'Really?'

Because if Sam hadn't cared enough to say

anything, to *feel* anything, then he didn't deserve
to have—

'Yes, *really*.' There was a sudden sharp edge
on her voice. 'I mean, I'm saying I don't know
because he didn't mention it specifically. Maybe
he *did* mind and kept it to himself, but I don't
think so. I mean, he knew we were friends, knew
you were on the other side of the world. He didn't
seem bothered, never seemed…' A shrug filled
her voice. 'He seemed cool.'

*Too cool for school! Cooler than him. Three
cheers for Sam the ice-man!*

He inhaled. 'Okay, then. That's good. Because
I'd hate to think that anything I did—'

'You didn't.' She sighed, and then her voice
was softening. 'It wasn't your fault, Alden, okay,
so please, don't go off on one.'

'Okay.'

And then the covers were tussling again. 'Can
we go to sleep now?'

She was shutting him down.

'Of course.'

He rolled onto his back. He hadn't meant to
touch a nerve but clearly, she was done talking
about it so, that was that.

He closed his eyes, felt his muscles starting
to loosen, a welcome heaviness stealing through
his limbs. For a blurry beat he felt a thought trying to surface, but then it was gone. Just as well.

Thoughts only kept him awake, and he was tired suddenly, ready to sleep.

He turned his head in her direction. 'Night night, Jules.'

'Night, Alden.'

CHAPTER TEN

'So, JULES, what is it that you do?'

Franc's smile was enigmatic, but his eyes were warm and interested. He really was everything Alden had said he would be. Kind. Courteous. Sensitive. Making sure that she didn't feel excluded from the breakfast conversation even though she was, curiously, the only partner here.

Maybe the other actors' partners had been invited too but couldn't come. Or hadn't wanted to come. *Understandable!* Although, to be fair, she was feeling lighter today now that she knew everyone.

And of course surviving their first night was definitely a weight off. She didn't even mind too much that Alden had been commandeered by the elderly and quite delightful Trudi Finch on their way out to the breakfast terrace and was now her prisoner on the opposite side of the table.

She set her cup down. 'I'm a florist.'

'Jules has her own shop in Richmond.' Alden

smiled over, a tangible note of pride in his voice. '"Wild Blooms".'

'Wild?' Natasha's eyebrows arched. 'So what is that? Unstructured arrangements, that kind of thing?'

In spite of herself, Jules found herself smiling. Natasha was not her favourite person, but the fact that she got the concept was a point in her favour.

'Exactly. I like flowers and foliage to look natural, as if I've just gathered them up—'

'But that's the skill, isn't it, making them *look* gathered…?' Alden again, cutting in, eyes locked on hers, glowing, and then he was looking around the table. 'You should see the way Jules puts things together. She does events and weddings, right! Takes an old barn or an old hall, and by the time she's finished it looks like a forest glade, or something enchanted, like a fairy tale.'

Pride in his voice. *Real.* Must be real, because she could feel warmth creeping into her cheeks, tears prickling behind her lids.

So many times, standing in her workroom, he'd said similar things but somehow, here, it was like hearing it for the first time: all the shades of admiration in his voice; all the colours burning in his gaze. It was a little bit overwhelming.

And there was a sense that everyone around the table could see how it was affecting her and she didn't necessarily like that, but at the same time, it was an opportunity, wasn't it, to bang the

drum for Alden, for how devoted he was, for how
solid they were—ergo how solid *he* was, the opposite of his perceived image. Hardly an acting
challenge, even for her, because he *was* solid,
was a devoted friend…

She pressed her fingers to her eyes, taking
her time so everyone would see, then she looked
around the table, feeling a sudden, unlikely smile
coming. 'Looks like I'm marrying my biggest
fan, doesn't it!'

There was a satisfying ripple of laughter, a
moment where she found herself caught in Alden's gaze, and then Franc was rising, dropping
his napkin onto the table.

'Marrying your biggest fan is always a good
idea, but right now I need to borrow him.' He
opened his gaze to the wider table. 'I need to
borrow you all. We must make a start!'

There was a surge of movement—cups being
drained, chairs scraping—and then Franc's eyes
came back, warm and, kind.

'Feel free to go foraging in the garden if you
want. You'll find secateurs in the storeroom next
to the kitchen, and vases. Ask Marie, my housekeeper, if you can't find what you need.'

'Thanks…' She felt a blush creeping. 'You're
very kind.'

Not that she had any intention of raiding his
borders. The thought of it appealed, for sure, but
the others might think she was showing off or,

worse, obliquely touting for business, and what if she didn't live up to her biggest fan's hype?

'Jules…?'

She looked up and her breath caught. Her biggest fan was making his way round the table, closing in, a strange, determined look in his eyes.

She shot him a smile. 'Hey, you—' But before anything else could come out, she was being drawn to her feet, kissed, and released.

For an eternal, thumping moment his eyes held hers, searching, taking her apart, and then a slight, pleased smile emerged. 'See you in a bit.'

And then he was turning, following the others into the house.

She stood, swaying, trying to draw in some air. *What was that?*

No prelude, just *boom!* A kiss too quick to taste, but a kiss all the same. And what about that look in his eyes, that little smile?

She lowered herself back into her seat, touching her lips, feeling for a trace, but there wasn't any. No tingle, no hum, just a rattling inside, but that was shock. Fading now. Giving way to a simple explanation. Obvious, really: he was her fake fiancé. She'd had an emotional moment at the table, caused by his obvious pride and deep affection. And he had seized the opportunity she created with her 'biggest fan' remark, picking up his cue, following through, *for show*.

Made sense. Because the kiss itself had been

brief, barely a kiss at all. Nothing to get lost in, tangled up about. A stunt!

She drew in a breath and reached for the cafetière, pouring herself a top-up. Some warning would have been good. A signalling look of some kind, like at the party when he'd kissed her forehead. She'd known that was coming because he'd told her with his eyes, and he'd taken his time, not jumped her unawares.

She lifted her cup, cradling it in her hands. She would have to say something. Kissing her forehead was fine, and she didn't mind a light hand on her back. Even a firm, possessive hand on her waist was acceptable fake-fiancé behaviour in certain circumstances, such as last night, when he'd interrupted her mid-flow with Hayden just as she'd been subtly interrogating him about his career.

Hayden *was* quite the dish, if you were into square-jawed, slick-haired types, and of course, he was uber-successful so, fair play, a fiancé might be expected to wade in in that situation. But kissing was not in the script. Not that they had one but, even so, Alden had to know—*must* know—that kissing her on the lips, even a short, sharp, highly charged kiss like that one, was pushing it by—

'Are you finished, *mademoiselle*?'

The softly spoken words made her start. Marie. Standing with a tray. Waiting to clear the table.

'Yes, thank you.' She set her cup down and rose to her feet. 'Would you like a hand?'

Because she was free, after all, and maybe doing something useful would help take her mind off the kiss. But the housekeeper's features crimped in horror.

'No, *mademoiselle*. You are a guest.' She was shaking her head. 'You are not here to work.'

'Okay.' She stepped aside, chastened. 'Thank you.'

Into the garden, then, to look around, see what was growing. Down the steps, away from the terrace, onto the lower path.

Franc had toured them this far when they arrived, but she'd been too preoccupied with the imminent viewing of their sleeping quarters to take it all in properly. She was seeing it now, though, bathed in soft morning sunshine, the vast grounds stretching away on all sides to thick woodland. Vast, yet secluded. Like all the other properties she'd glimpsed on those madly twisting roads they'd taken yesterday.

Clearing the city, climbing higher, the view had, perversely, narrowed. Dense trees, flashes of white stucco through tall gates, a suggestion of pantiles over high walls. And inside those walls, there must have been homes like this one. Elegantly proportioned, with tall windows and ornate balconies. With sheltered terraces for dining, rampant with bougainvillea and heady jasmine.

With neatly clipped lawns, ornamental hedges, and deep, colourful borders. Pristine turquoise swimming pools. Neatly white-lined tennis courts. Everything lovely…

But not quite lovely enough to stop her mind going back to that kiss. Because even though it had been a stunt, it was an extraordinary one to pull out of the blue like that.

That determined trajectory around the table; that deep, unswerving gaze. It had felt off-the-charts exhilarating. Heart-stopping, breath-catching, blood-tingling.

And now her heart was speeding up again, bouncing against her ribcage, and it had no business doing that, pumping hard because of a kiss that didn't matter, that didn't mean anything.

She scrubbed at her lips. All this quivering confusion because her friend—*friend, remember*—was a brilliant actor!

She drew in a deep breath and forced her feet forward. That Alden *was* such a brilliant actor did throw up one tantalising silver lining, though, a slightly wicked one, but hell, she wasn't a saint. If Natasha had noticed the kiss—and surely, she must have—she might be feeling a bit jealous right now, a bit irked, and that was satisfying, because Natasha had well and truly irked *her* last night, hadn't she? Going on like that about Alden's parents, faking her wide-eyed concern at their ongoing lack of support. As if she knew anything about it, as if she knew what he'd been through over the years, how tormented, how confounded he'd felt, how...

Stop it, Jules!

She stepped off the path and sank down onto the grass, staring through the wire mesh fence at the clay surface of the tennis court in front of her. This wasn't about Natasha. Oh, she'd thought so last night, but it wasn't Natasha she was mad at. It was Alden.

She didn't like that he had shared those things with Natasha which, she knew, was off-the-scale unreasonable. He'd been with Natasha for five months, after all. And even if they'd had 'intense sexual chemistry', as Natasha claimed, they must have talked as well. Of course they had. Alden was a talker. He couldn't hold a thought in his head for more than five minutes at a time. He might not have got as far as outlining all of his friendships—*theirs*—but of course he would have told Natasha about his family.

And she'd got herself feeling all put out about it, jealous, because she had always cherished the notion that *she* was the one he talked to, turned to. *The only one.* Because he was *her* only one, wasn't he? And she'd wanted them to be the same, liked the idea of it, clung to it, because it made her feel special, treasured. But it was stupid.

Insane! And if she hadn't cloistered herself

up, staying out of his world so thoroughly—if she hadn't kept staring at him through her rose-tinted, one-dimensional lens—she would have acknowledged to herself by now that he opened up to other people, especially to his girlfriends. Because why wouldn't he? That was what people in love did, how they became closer. It was just her who didn't.

Couldn't...

She felt a lump thickening in her throat, tears starting to prickle.

Alden had asked her if Sam minded him calling in the night, and she'd felt caught out, hadn't she? Irritated. Because she didn't know. Hadn't known. Because the truth was that she'd never really been tuned into Sam. Not in her heart. Not in the way that mattered.

Not in the way he wanted.

She dropped her head into her hands.

Those bruised eyes on hers, angry, and pleading, wet at the edges.

'What am I for, Jules?'

If not to be loved, if not to have your full attention, if not to be your best friend, the one you need twenty-four-seven, not just to hold you at night?

She bit down on her lip, swallowing hard. He hadn't said those things, but he might as well have, because that was why he'd left, calling her out with that parting shot. Because she'd only

ever skimmed his surface, hadn't she, allowed
him to skim hers. Always the same with her. She
was a freak who couldn't push past the shallows.
How did people even do that, go deep with other
people, when people always left eventually?

Like Mum. Even Mum left and mums weren't
supposed to do that, ever! And she wasn't one of
those kids who took it on herself, blamed herself,
felt that she'd deserved to be abandoned because
of something she had done. No way. It wasn't
her fault, or Dad's, or Emily's. It was squarely
Mum's, for deciding that the grass was greener
elsewhere.

And who knew? Not her, because she didn't
talk to her any more, but maybe Mum's grass
was greener now. And maybe she was happy.
And maybe that was just the way life went, some
people putting themselves first, others having to
suck it up.

Well, she *had* sucked it up, hadn't she, with
Alden's help, smoothed it all out. She'd got on
with her life, found arms to fall into. Boys at
school, then men. Lovely men like Sam, who
stayed for a while, long enough to fool her into
thinking that she was good at relationships.

But she wasn't. She was a serial failure. Because of the scar inside that wouldn't heal, that
wouldn't quite flatten. A little raised bit, a little
bit of resistance rising up, like the fence around
this tennis court. She'd looked through it, never

properly noticing it, never making sense of it, until this moment.

But now she could see it, clear as day: she didn't let herself go with people, didn't let them in, because of Mum. Because she didn't want to hurt like that, didn't want to feel that broken and betrayed ever again. *Oh, God!* The irony was almost laughable. *She* was the one who was incapable of love!

She wiped her eyes, slow-breathing to calm herself, letting the thought settle. It scanned, made sense and yet—she felt her chest tightening—it didn't *feel* right. If she was incapable of love, then why did she keep trying to find it? Absolutely, she craved physical affection, but it didn't begin and end with that. When she started out with someone new, it was because there was something in his eyes, a promise there, something that ignited a little flame of hope in her heart. It wouldn't ignite, wouldn't burn, if she couldn't love. It just wouldn't!

She leaned back onto her hands, lifting her face to the lulling warmth of the sun. So maybe trust was the issue, not the heart. Hard to trust anyone when the one person who was supposed to love you more than anything in the world had found it in herself to just up and leave.

If only Mum had talked to her, forewarned her, confided in her about the other man, then, yes, it would still have hurt but maybe not as much, and maybe now they would at least see each other from time to time. But Mum had gone for the nuclear option, and there was no coming back from that kind of devastation.

She closed her eyes, watching the sun spangles dancing behind her lids. Nothing Mum could say or do now to fix things, but she could choose to draw a line under Mum, couldn't she? Stop the stain from spreading further? She was only twenty-nine years old—*not* a lost cause. She could take herself in hand, work on her issues now that she knew what they were.

Or was she doing an Alden, overthinking everything, seeing issues where there weren't any? Maybe her 'problem'—in inverted commas— was simply that she hadn't met the right person yet! When that happened, surely she'd know, feel it beating inside, feel trust and love flowing out like a river? It wasn't as if she didn't have an inkling of how it ought to feel, because it felt like that with Alden.

She felt a frown coming. It did most of the time anyway. But now this stupid fake engagement was skewing everything, straining at old ropes, unleashing inappropriate feelings. Desires. And that out-of-the-blue kiss wasn't helping one little bit, even though it had been a meaningless stunt.

She rocked forward off her hands blinking the spangles away. She couldn't let herself think about it—that look in his eyes as he drew her to her feet, that cryptic smile afterwards. He'd explain later, no doubt, and it would all stack up, and they would probably laugh about it, and then everything would feel normal again.

She got to her feet, smoothing her dress down. In the meantime, there was this lovely garden…

CHAPTER ELEVEN

HE TOOK THE steps down from the terrace, re-tracing the route they'd taken with Franc the day before. Not that Jules was likely to be in the vicinity still. She'd set off this way after breakfast, the housekeeper said, but the grounds were vast. She could be anywhere by now.

He plodded on, loafers crunching on the loose shingle, scanning the lawns and the trees beyond. Anywhere was fine by him. He could use the walk, frankly, and he didn't mind looking. The problem would come once he found her because then he was going to have to explain that kiss.

He felt his stomach tightening for the hundredth time since breakfast. Luckily, Caspar wasn't in the early scenes, so he'd been able to tune out a bit, think things through, come up with an explanation that would hopefully stack up.

Jules had conjured a very convincing show of emotion in the wake of his praise for her artistry, then come out with a very sweet and amusing quip. She'd had them all eating out of her hand,

and because he'd been sitting across the table, instead of next to her, he couldn't touch her shoulder, or kiss her hair and so, because the emotion of the moment demanded it, because there had been a weight of expectation gathering around that table, he'd had to go for high drama.

He stopped, ran his eyes over the tennis court. *Stupid, Alden!*

This was literally the last place Jules would hang out. And she wouldn't be in the pool or sunbathing on the surrounding terrace. The sun was too hot at this time of day, too intense.

He turned himself towards the trees, stepping out. Jules liked trees, and deep green shade. Odds were she would be in there, communing with the foliage. He'd comb the woods, find her, explain himself, and then he was going to take her out for the afternoon, to some little town with cobbled streets and thronging bistros and all the appropriate vibes. And maybe on those bustling streets he'd find his friend Jules again and forget he knew how her lips tasted.

He broke shade and stopped, heart drumming. *Oh, God!* But how did you forget a thing like that, switch off the yearning when it was mounting inside, burning?

He rubbed his head, swallowing a groan, then forced his feet to move. All his own fault. He should never have poured himself out like that at the table: all the admiration he had inside for

Jules. Even as he was saying the words, he'd felt his old teenage susceptibilities resurrecting themselves, tugging him towards trouble.

But he couldn't stop himself from talking because she was amazing, and she would only have played down her talent, as she always did, keeping that bit of reserve about her that she'd acquired after Paulina rode off into the sunset— and he hadn't wanted that. He'd wanted them all to see her as he did, felt it like a mission, whirring like a dynamo inside, unstoppable.

And then she'd made everyone laugh with that deft one-liner and he'd thought he was going to burst. She was his friend, *being* the best friend a person could have, painting him as the devoted fiancé, which was exactly what they'd planned, but in that moment, he couldn't see his friend. All he could see was her lovely face, wet-eyed, shy-smiling, and he'd wanted to hold her, kiss her, wanted it so much it hurt.

And of course he was going to tell her he'd kissed her for show, for the audience, because how could he possibly say anything else? But the truth was, by the time he'd extricated himself from Trudi's clutches, he couldn't rightly say if there'd been anyone left at the table to see. All he'd wanted was for Jules to feel the depth of his admiration, the aching tenderness he was feeling inside.

Thank God he'd snapped to his senses quickly,

though. He could make a fleeting kiss fit the story he was going to tell. Oh, but it didn't mean he wasn't feeling it, *living* it over and over again: the sweet, soft, shock of her mouth; her up-close scent; the startled blue of her eyes that flickered a kaleidoscope in that afterwards moment, a kaleidoscope that had warmed him to the core, lifted him, made him smile...

He paused, scanning the trees for a splash of yellow sundress—Jules's favourite colour—but there was nothing ahead except leafy green and glinting sunshine.

He pushed on, heart drumming. He couldn't let himself wonder about that kaleidoscope in her eyes. To wonder about it would be fatal, would lead him seriously astray, and wasn't he in enough trouble already? For sure, they hadn't talked about boundaries, or set any, but instinctively he knew that kissing Jules on the mouth was off-limits. And yet it hadn't stopped him, had it? And afterwards her eyes had seemed to...

Stop!

Hadn't he just told himself *not* to slide, *not* to wonder? Wondering was open-ended, malleable. Facts weren't, so maybe it was time to face them. Tough love and all that!

If Jules had ever been interested him in that way, then something would have happened between them years ago. She would have nudged his foot back with a lifted eyebrow, maybe touched his hand. Or in the park that day, celebrating ElastiMan, champagne-dizzy on that rug with the warm sun breathing down their necks, she might have put her hand on his shoulder, holding it there, holding his gaze with a deep look. But she hadn't and that was because he was patently *not* her type. Right from school, she had always gone for tall, dark-haired guys.

Like Hayden...

He felt his jaw tighten. Last night was proof enough of that! Talking to Hayden for ages, smiling, sparkling at him. If she hadn't been 'engaged' to *him*, all sandy-haired, goofy-grinned, five-foot-ten-and-half inches of him, who knew what could have happened?

Oh, God! And now he was winding himself up, feeling jealous, when all of it was completely *irrelevant*.

Jules was his friend.

His best friend.

They were cemented into that shape. Had been for years. And it was easy, comfortable, completely brilliant. Definitely for the best. Because in spite of all the notches on his bed post, he was still as clueless as ever about women, routinely prone to messing up. Jules was a risk he could absolutely *not* afford to take, a person he could *not* bear to lose.

Especially since she'd only come here for *his* sake, to keep him focused and level-headed so

he could impress Franc and get the Saul part
if Hayden chucked it in. And now, because of
a stupid impulse, he wasn't only the opposite
of focused and level-headed, but he'd probably
confused the hell out of her too. Probably that
was why she was out here tramping through the
woods. She was trying to make sense of her idi-
otic friend!

He stopped to draw breath, to let the tightness
inside melt away.

This must be the north-east side of the prop-
erty. The white gable of the house was just visible
through the trees together with a small portion of
the rear elevation, a modern, single-storey addi-
tion that housed the gym and the sauna and the
laundry.

And then, suddenly, a whisper slid into his ear
from behind.

'Boo!'

'What the—?' He spun round, heart going,
but then laughter was taking him, springing him
loose.

Jules was standing a foot or two away, her face
a study in impishness.

'Sorry, but you were easy prey. I couldn't resist.'
She smiled. 'What are you doing here?'

How could she not know?

'I was looking for you.'

'Ah!' Her eyes lit. 'It's a good job I found you
then because otherwise it would have been a

fruitless mission. The woods go on for ever that way—' she gestured ahead '—all the way over to the other side. I was on my way back but then I saw you, thought it would be fun to circle round, give you a little fright.'

He clapped a hand to his chest to tease her. 'Nice!'

She folded her arms. 'Oh, switch off that wounded look. If you'd seen me first, you'd have totally done the same thing.'

'Wouldn't.'

'Would.'

'Wouldn't...'

Expanding silence.

Ought he to dive in, explain about the kiss? The air itself seemed to demand it, but at the same time it didn't feel like quite the right moment. Or maybe he was just a coward. Either way, small talk was suggesting itself.

He licked his lips. 'I was looking for you because Franc's finished with us for today...'

Her chin lifted. 'Ah!'

'Shall we walk?'

Because moving was bound to feel better than standing like this, twitching at the end of her gaze.

'Sure.' She smiled, falling in beside him. 'So, afternoon off, then?'

He nodded. 'Franc says he's easing us in gently, but actually I think he's got a meeting after lunch, then some video calls to make later this afternoon. You know how it is with the time difference to LA...'

'*I* do, yes.'

Emphasising the 'I', sliding her eyebrow up. *Teasing.*

'*Touché*, dearest one.'

He felt relief unfurling with his smile. Playfulness was just the ticket. Except that now he'd brought up LA, last night was thundering back. That Sam conversation. That thought, eluding him before he could seize it. Some fragment. Shifting again, rising, taking shape...

He'd asked Jules about Sam because he'd hated the thought of being even a little bit responsible for Sam leaving, because of the pain it had caused her, but at the same time, could he deny that a part of him had wanted to hear her say that Sam *had* minded him calling in the wee small hours? Because she always picked up, didn't she, and if Sam had minded, but she was picking up anyway, then it could only mean that she put him above Sam, and wrong as that was, unfair to Sam as that was, he really, really liked the idea of that...

But apparently Sam had seemed cool about his calls.

He felt a frown coming. Still didn't get that! How could Sam *not* have been bothered? Unless it was exactly as Jules said: that Sam had accepted their friendship, hadn't seen him as any kind of threat. Which he hadn't been. Of course.

He felt his belly tightening. Still, it wouldn't have done for *him*. If Jules had been his, he'd have had something to say about late-night callers. Then again, if Jules had been his, she'd have been having far too good a time in bed with him to want to get out of it in the middle of the night.

Gah!

And now he was losing himself in a completely inappropriate, hypothetical projection when he was supposed to be steadying the wheel, paving his way towards explaining the kiss...

He caught her eye. 'So anyway, because unlike me Franc is on top of his time zones, the rest of the afternoon is ours. I think the others are having a late lunch here, but I promised you *funshine*, so what do you say to us taking off? We can brave the scary roads, go exploring, find a bistro...'

She came to sudden halt. 'That sounds lovely, but first can we talk about the elephant in the woods?'

His heart plummeted. Beating him to it. Always three steps ahead. And now he was on the back foot. *Why* hadn't he dealt with it straight away, so she didn't have to? Why was he so weak, so useless?

With an effort, he mustered a confident tone. 'I was going to get to that.'

Her eyes held his, for once unreadable.

He felt a flick of panic. 'Are you mad? Cross, I mean?'

'No, of course not.' Her expression softened. 'But I would like an explanation…'

He felt relief pumping through. 'Not cross' was good.

He pushed his hands though his hair, trying and failing to remember his script. 'It just fitted the moment, that's all.'

'Fitted the moment?' For a second her focus turned inwards. 'I can see that, but some warning would have been helpful.'

'I couldn't warn you because it wasn't premeditated. It sort of, evolved.'

Her eyes narrowed a little, prompting, but he didn't need prompting. Suddenly the words were coming in a rush.

'When Franc asked you what you did, I knew you'd close it down the first chance you got because you always do and, I don't know, I suppose I just wanted them all to know how great you are, how talented, so I jumped in, and then you turned on the emotion—which was a terrific piece of theatre, by the way—and then, oh my God, that cute thing you said about marrying your biggest fan… That pulled it together like a sweet knot.

'If I'd been sitting next you, I'd have hugged you, or kissed you on the head or something, but there was that time lag because I was opposite, and I could feel a sort of expectant buzz and, I suppose having to come round to your side meant that there was already a forward motion happening—a momentum, if you like—and I'm sorry if it threw you, but it just felt like the right thing to do...' *Breathe and rephrase...* 'What I mean is, it felt as if everyone was expecting me to do it.'

She was silent for a moment and then her eyebrows flicked up. 'Well, I suppose you never have been one to let an audience down.'

He felt a protest rising and swallowed it. Telling her that he'd kissed her because he wanted to and not because of the audience, kissed her because he hadn't been able to stop himself, wouldn't serve any purpose. It would only confuse things, cross more wires. Even so, he couldn't bear her to think that the feelings that had led him to it weren't genuine.

'I try not to, but Jules, what I said to them, about how great you are, how talented you are with the flowers and everything... You know I meant it, right?'

Her gaze fell. When it came back, it was wet at the edges.

'Of course I do because you say it all the time.' And then she was pressing her fingers to her eyes, smiling a bit. 'God, here I go again, getting emotional.' She drew in a noisy breath. 'Hearing you say it in front of everyone was really touching, though.'

Her eyes were soft on his, gleaming. 'And, for the record, I wasn't faking. It wasn't a piece of theatre. I already told you, I'm not Greta Garbo. What you see is what you get.' Her hands went to her face again, wiping. 'It was pure luck that that line popped into my head. As you say, it worked like a dream.'

He felt warmth blooming in his chest. 'Dream team.'

She smiled and suddenly an urge was muscling in, strong, and pure, but he couldn't let himself act on it, not without permission.

'Jules…can I give you a hug?'

She blinked, surprised, and then her smile widened. 'I don't see why not. It sort of fits the moment.'

And then he moved, and she moved, and she was in his arms, snuggling in, all soft and warm. He held her tight, breathing her in, not wanting to let go because the feeling was too sublime, but not letting go would change the landscape, and it was hard enough keeping tabs on his emotions in this one.

'Right…' With difficulty he loosened his hold, releasing her, trying to sound casual, unaffected. 'Shall we hit the road—see stuff?'

'Sounds perfect.' She stepped back, a little flushed, a little breathless, and then her eyes lifted to his, a familiar light shining that seemed to say that they were back on track. 'I've always wanted to see *stuff*.'

CHAPTER TWELVE

SHE FELT HER breath catching, then a fizzing rush of delight. Pink umbrellas! As far as the eye could see. Rows and rows of them, suspended above the street, dancing on wires, throwing fat polka-dot shadows onto the ground, filling every window with bobbing pink reflections.

She looked at Alden. His sunglasses were glinting pink too, but his smile was white, and as wide and electric as ever.

'I was *not* expecting this.' He was shaking his head. 'It's like bunting on speed...'

She felt a second rush. Happiness this time. Because they were together, having fun, which was exactly what he'd promised.

They'd left Franc's an hour ago, taking it in turns to choose roads on the basis of pure whim: *follow that car, that dog, that cyclist!* And now they were here, in a little town called Grasse, hungry and on the hunt for a nice little bistro. But the streets were so narrow that it had felt wise to park the car and walk.

Up a steep, cobbled street with the sun beating down, following the Centre Ville sign, and then they'd turned the corner into this sweet surprise.

She pulled out her phone, took a shot. 'It's so pretty.'

'Yeah. But I'm not seeing any bistros.'

He was right. The establishments on both sides were shops, mundane ones at that: an ironmonger, a pharmacy, a travel shop. A branch of Crédit Agricole.

'Let's go.' He was beckoning her on. 'We need to find the chintzy square where the restaurants are before we starve to death.'

She fell in beside him, holding in a smile. Alden was nearly always hungry. Full of nervous energy, burning it up, running hot. Like in the woods at Franc's, visibly pent up because of the kiss, but blocked for some reason, so that she'd had to raise it, shake it out of him. And it was exactly as she'd thought: a kiss to fit the moment, a show-kiss for the crowd…

She felt a tingle. Except… There hadn't actually been a crowd, had there? Couldn't have been because hadn't she watched him walk away, going through the door *after* everyone else?

Her heart pulsed. So what did that mean?

What do you want it to mean?

She flicked him a glance.

Strolling along, sunglasses glinting. That gorgeous thatch of hair, that lovely mouth framing a hint of smile, enough to put happy little dents in his cheeks.

She felt a tug inside, the old confusion stirring. *Oh, God...* That light in his eyes afterwards, that smile... Was there any possibility that the kiss had been real? Had he kissed her because he wanted to? Was that why he'd been so unforthcoming in the woods, not getting to his explanation straight away because he was all at sea, unsure of what to say, of what *she* might say...?

If only the kiss had lasted a bit longer, she could have taken the measure of it, better discerned the intention behind it.

Or was she just looking, hoping, for intention because every moment they were together felt better than the moment before? Because every time he smiled into her eyes, she could feel something trilling through her veins? Awareness. Pulsing excitement. As if something was changing. Happening. About to.

Stop it, Jules!

Reading into looks, smiles, gestures; taking them apart, putting them back together again with a different spin: she was becoming as bad as Alden. Turning herself inside out like he did. And for what? Because if it had come to it, if he had tried to kiss her for longer, would she have let him? Would she let him if it came to it again, risk that kind of intimacy with her friend—*her best friend*—the one person she couldn't bear to—

'After you, sweetness.'

She blinked. He was standing aside with an impish grin, directing her along a tight alley that opened onto a narrow pedestrianised street lined with small, vibrant shops and, overhead, more bright pink umbrellas.

She passed through, slowing so he could catch up. All the questions. No answers. Because everything was different here. Sights, sounds, smells. Even the air seemed—

'What is *that*?'

Alden, beside her again, looking up, pulling off his sunglasses.

She followed his gaze to the fine black tube running across the street above them. It was spurting out mist, a curiously sweet-smelling mist.

She felt her brow furrowing. 'I have no idea.'

'C'est parfum.'

The voice belonged to a woman who was busy slotting fat paper cones of tied lavender into a display basket outside a tiny shop that seemed to be a shrine to lavender. She stopped, assessing them with a quick, beady gaze, and then she smiled. 'It's perfume. Grasse is famous...' Her hands raked the air as she searched for the words. 'Famous...in all the world...for perfume.'

'Ah!' Alden's eyes came to hers with an accompanying comedy grimace. 'Maybe we should have bought a Riviera guidebook.' And then he was smiling at the woman, pointing at the lavender. 'So, is Grasse famous for lavender too?'

'Bien sûr, monsieur.' This was accompanied with profuse nodding and a great deal of gesticulating at the displays. 'Famous for rose. Famous for lavender.'

'In that case, I should buy some.'

The woman's eyes met hers briefly, darted to her left hand, and then she was looking at Alden again. 'For your fiancée?' Her eyebrows lifted approvingly. *'Vous êtes un romantique, non?'*

'Romantic? Me?' He chuckled, looking over. 'You'd better ask her!'

As if she would know. But she couldn't not play the game now that it was somehow in progress. On this tiny street in Grasse. With a complete stranger.

She broke away from his gaze and smiled at the woman. 'Oh, yes. *Oui!* He is *très romantique.*' She pressed her hands to her chest, faking a swoon. 'He takes me to the finest restaurants and he always…*toujours*…orders champagne for me…*champagne*…because I love it.'

She could sense him laughing silently, could feel a giggle vibrating, but the woman's eyes were holding her fast, busy with translating, and it was simply too delicious a temptation to resist, beyond impossible not to want to stitch him up completely.

She widened her eyes into the woman's gaze.

'He sings to me as well. You know…?' She felt her own hands going, her brain searching for fragments of school French. *'Chanter. Il chant… chansons d'amour.'*

'Ah!' The woman transferred her gaze to Alden. 'You are a *chanteur*?' Her brows drew in. 'Are you famous?' She was scrutinising his face, and then her finger went up with a sharp intake of breath. *'Je vous connais…'* More peering. 'I know you…'

'No.' Alden was shaking his head, digging into a pocket for his wallet. *'Non, non, non!'* He shrugged his shoulders. *'Je suis…not* a singer. *Not* famous.'

His eyes flicked over, signalling SOS.

She bit down on her lip hard, trying to swallow the laughter that was boiling in her belly. She couldn't speak, didn't dare to, in case she exploded. All she could do was watch him handing over his euros, protesting his anonymity all over again to the woman's colleague who had now come out of the shop to give him the once-over.

Sandy hair. Sunglasses parked. Boyish smile. Linen shirt. Three-quarter cargoes. Tanned calves, tan loafers.

She felt a tug, a little tingle starting.

Yes. Everything was different here. The air. The streets. The people. What they did with umbrellas. So why not the two of them?

Why not them?

They were out of context, unbottled, so if she

was feeling new things, seeing new things in him, then it could be the same for him too. Last night in bed, hadn't he said that he was feeling weird? They'd both said it. So there it was! They were both feeling weird, experiencing patches of turbulence between these kinds of moments which were their normal. Fun scrapes. Teasing and nonsense.

She drew in a breath, reconnecting with the scene. Alden, clutching the bouquet with one hand, trying to extricate himself with the other. She felt her lips twitching.

Turbulence made sense. And so did this: Alden admired her. He loved her, as a friend. In his eyes all the time, such as just now, alongside that silent distress call. Such as after that unexpected hug in the woods. Warm, tight, sweet as a sigh, but only for a moment, because it *was* just a hug. A full stop to punctuate the end of their heart-to-heart.

And just because there had been no one left sitting at the table by the time he drew her to her feet and kissed her, it didn't mean that he hadn't felt, or been propelled by, that weight of expectation he'd talked about, felt it all the way round the table to her side. Another patch of turbulence. It stacked up. Absolutely.

Sort of.

Oh, God!

She *had* to let it go, stop thinking about it because Alden was turning away from the women now, and his eyes were fastening on hers, baleful but twinkling.

He waved the lavender under her nose then put it into her hands. 'Here you are, minx, although I'm not sure you deserve it.'

'I totally deserve it.' She aimed a 'thank you' smile at the women, who were still looking at them, then turned, pulling at his arm so he'd come along. 'You put the ball in my court, and I furnished you with an enviable array of romantic credentials.'

'What, a champagne-sized wallet and a penchant for singing?'

He was smiling wryly, triggering a little sunburst inside.

She loved this, the way they set to, loved the bubbly feeling she got when she was thinking of what to say, thinking of how to draw him on and make him laugh, that tingling anticipation of how he was going to answer. Just talking, but elevated somehow, thrilling...

'Well, you *can* sing.' She felt a giggle rising. 'I mean, I didn't totally hate you in *Oklahoma!*'

'That must make you the only one, then, not that I'm bitter or anything.'

'It was a school production! Rubbish sounddesk! And I suspect Holly and Craig were guzzling alcopops on the sly, because Mr Chapman wasn't supervising. He was chatting up Miss Creely in the wings, which I could see from the front row, by the way. So no wonder the sound levels were all over the place. Music teacher AWOL. So-called sound engineers on the sauce. You didn't stand a chance.'

'So my dodgy baritone had nothing to do with it, then?' He laughed roundly. 'You're too kind.'

'I thought I was a minx.'

'You're that as well.' His eyes came to hers, all warm. 'You can be more than one thing, you know.'

Oh, she knew that all right, because at this moment she was so many things. Happy, because they were together, having fun. Shocked, because she was somehow still holding his arm, feeling its warmth pulsing into her palm, the hard swell of his biceps not remotely pulling away. Fluttery, because they seemed to be slowing down and his gaze was intensifying again, same as on the bed, same as over the table that morning…

Turbulence.

Thrilling, but unsettling: a storm to ride or, prelude to a devastating crash…

She shuddered inwardly and let go of his arm, slipping a smile into her voice to make it sound light and breezy. 'You mean like hungry *and* thirsty?'

His eyes clouded for a split second and then he dropped his sunglasses over them with a smile. 'Exactly!' He turned, scanning the street ahead.

'Up there looks promising for restaurants, although I can't guarantee that they'll be the finest.'

'Hey, that was my alter ego speaking, your *enamoured* fiancée…' Saying the words out loud felt important. Cathartic. 'You know very well that in the real world I'm happy with a beer and a hotdog.'

He scanned the menu. They might *be* in the real world—or at least in a weird alternative version of it, where things about Jules that he shouldn't be noticing were constantly catching him out, such as how smooth her bare arms were and how her breasts swelled just so under the neckline of her sundress—but that didn't mean she had to settle for beer.

It was what they usually drank together—that or wine, if they were having pasta—but maybe she'd mentioned champagne before because she fancied some today. She'd seemed to enjoy it at Franc's party, after all, and it wasn't as if he couldn't afford it.

He wasn't banking megastar fees yet but, thanks to Jacklyn's considerable negotiating skills, he was doing all right. A couple of popcorn movies a year at the leading end of the cast brought in decent money, and there was more voiceover work coming in these days. He was being considered for lead voice in *Back to the Mousehole*, which would be tidy if it came off. And next week he was shooting in Egypt, another popcorn movie, but this time he was playing the baddie, posturing and glowering in the desert. Not a stretch but a pleasant change. And, with two potential sequels on the cards, it could turn out to be lucrative.

But, even it if it wasn't, if Jules wanted to drink champagne then he wanted her to have it.

He looked over, felt a smile coming. She was scrutinising her menu, twirling a lock of hair around her finger, mouthing the French words to herself. So funny, watching her with that lavender woman, hands juggling the air, eyebrows going, trying to oil the rusty French wheels.

Charmante!

He felt his smile widening, taking over his cheeks. 'Seriously, if you'd like some champagne...?'

Her eyes lifted, holding him in an affectionate gaze. 'That's very sweet of you, but I'm not drinking champagne on my own. In fact, as your co-driver, I feel duty bound to drink Perrier, because we're going to need two clear heads if we're ever going to find our way back to Franc's.'

He pictured the radical bends overhung with trees; reckless moments of blinding sunshine and deep shade; barrelling, full-tilt vehicles...

'You make a fair point.'

She directed her gaze to the menu for a scant second. 'Besides, even though it's probably sacrilegious, I want a pizza, and I'm sure champagne doesn't go with pizza.'

'Pizza isn't sacrilegious. If it was, it wouldn't be on the menu, and if it wasn't on the menu then we'd be moving on, because it's what you want.'

'That's very noble…' Her lips twitched minutely, kick-starting a chuckle low down in his belly and then she was dipping her chin, fixing him with wry look. 'You want pizza too, right?'

He let it go, laughing. 'Totally!'

Always reading him.

But then the laughter was dying, and his chest was going tight. Had she read him on the street back there, seen the desire inside? Her hand on his arm, that sweet warmth coming through his shirt sleeve, firing triggers… She didn't usually hold his arm, but then he didn't usually kiss her, did he? And what about that hug?

All things they didn't usually do.

He felt his heart twisting. But he'd wanted to kiss her, wanted to hold her, because they *were* the dream team and words could only express so much. Sometimes the soul cried out for more. And she'd flowed into his arms so readily in those woods, the way she did when she was aching over some guy. Except this time she'd been holding him *for himself* and not because he was a leaning post.

'*Salût, monsieur, madame…* Can I take your order?'

The waiter was young and brisk. Within moments he was back with a bottle of sparkling water, pouring it with a flourish, promising that their pizzas wouldn't be long.

'Cheers.' Jules chinked her glass to his then parked her elbows on the table, surveying the people around them as she always did.

He set his glass down, watching the bubbles rising, trying to reconnect his thoughts.

Maybe hugging had opened them up somehow, smashed through the 'do not touch' barrier that had always seemed to exist between them. Certainly, when she'd taken hold of his arm it had felt seamless, as natural as breathing.

And suddenly there he'd been, living his teenage dream, walking along with her all close as if they were a proper couple. Too tantalising a current not to get caught up in. No wonder he'd felt himself sliding into the danger zone, and she must have seen it—*must have*—because suddenly she had been removing her hand, jolting him back to reality.

But there was still this lagging confusion. Because she *had* taken his arm and held on, and there *had* been something in her eyes, a new, different sort of light shining. Or maybe it was wishful thinking.

Wishful?

His heart thumped. Wishing. Wanting. What did he want—Jules to be in love with him? Or was this tingling chaos he could feel inside just the remnant of an old dream that was sprouting new wings because of the situation, because they were together in a different place, at a table on a leafy street in Grasse with sun glinting on the glassware and a faint breeze playing with the edges of the tablecloth?

He lifted his gaze, catching hers on its way to somewhere over his shoulder. If so, he only had himself to blame. He'd known from the outset that being with her like this would be a torment as well as a pleasure. That face—the brimming life in it—undid him all the time: smiling cheeks; eyes prone to sparkling at the drop of a hat; those dark, agile brows; that sweet, wide curve of her mouth…

She was lovelier now than she'd ever been, and he wasn't a sad sixteen-year-old virgin any more. He couldn't stop his mind from churning out fantasies, seemingly couldn't stop himself from dancing close to the edge, feeling its magnet pull. But what if he did cross that line, didn't manage to stop himself next time? And what if she let him?

Oh, God! What then? Because he was an utter failure at relationships, wasn't he? Chasing after Natasha like a lovesick teenager yet somehow failing to supply her with the love she needed. And now he was, what, crushing on his best friend?

He picked up his glass, knocking back a mouthful. He could always do the fashionable thing,

blame his parents. Starving him of approval so
that he was always hungry, always suggestible,
jumping at every gun—always the wrong ones.
Somehow always choosing the wrong women,
women he couldn't make things last with. Would
things be different with Jules? And if they turned
out not to be, who could he blame then?

His heart seized. Who would he run to then?

And then suddenly her gleeful voice was snap-
ping him back like elastic.

'Alden, look!'

He twisted round and, in spite of himself, felt
a smile breaking.

A bright yellow tourist train full of happy pas-
sengers was coming up the pedestrianised street
towards them.

Totally Jules's kind of thing.

'"Le petit train des parfums".' She was reading the banner, doing a French accent. 'The little perfume train. Oh! It's stopping…' Sparkling
eyes came to his. 'Isn't it sweet?'

'Adorable.' He felt her pleasure infecting him,
pulling him out of his own head. 'Do you want
to go for a ride?'

'No.' She waggled her eyebrows at him. 'I
want my pizza.' And then she grinned. 'I'd love
a picture, though.' She pulled out her phone. 'Do
you mind?'

'Of course not.' He got to his feet, went round
to pull out her chair, doing his best not to look

at her smooth, bare shoulders. 'We'll call it, "girl in yellow dress with yellow train".'

'How very modernist!' She turned, smiling, putting her phone into his hand. 'Take one of me on my own first, so I can send it to Dad and Emily, then we'll do a selfie. We can call that one "Alden Phillips and fiancée shun Eurostar in favour of eco-friendly alternative".'

He laughed, feeling lighter, better. 'Witty! You know, if the floristry thing doesn't work out, there's always copywriting.'

CHAPTER THIRTEEN

'NOW, THERE'S A dental disaster in the making!'

Great slabs of nougat. Stacked high in the little shop window. Amazing to see but Alden wasn't wrong. She could almost feel her teeth aching.

'I agree. The patisserie in that other window was much more tempting.'

'Do you want to go back and get some?' He looked amused and vaguely incredulous. 'I mean, if you're still hungry…'

'How could I still be hungry after that huge pizza?' She tugged his sleeve to pull him away from the window. 'I was merely saying that the patisserie *looked* more appetising.'

'Ah.' He smiled. 'Okay.'

She felt her heart filling. He was in 'your wish is my command' mode, doing everything he'd promised. Looking after her. Did she want champagne? Did she want to ride on the train? Did she want patisserie on top of pizza? Meanwhile her hands were filled with his lavender bouquet which, whatever he said, did feel sort of romantic because he'd just gone right ahead and bought it, hadn't he? Spontaneously.

She adjusted her hands around it, flicking him a glance. He was making it easy to imagine how it would feel to be his girlfriend. All this attention. *Attentiveness*. Except, if she were his girlfriend, there would be the physical stuff too. Kissing. Not just a peck, but warm and lingering, slow enough to taste, to feel that soft grain of his tongue against hers, stroking, exploring. It would feel tender at first, oh, but then the levers would start tumbling, unlocking, and everything would be opening, drawing them in, onwards, making the fever come, and she would be tasting his skin, his throat, feeling his mouth on her neck, warm hands roaming, slipping under…and she would let her hands loose, run them over the firm swell of his shoulders, feeling that vibrant heat. Then she'd go for his buttons, undoing them one by—

'Jules…?'

His face snapped into focus, bemused, faintly quizzical.

Had he been trying to get her attention for a while?

She felt her cheeks tingling, prickling. Thank God for her shades, big enough to hide a multitude of sins.

'I'm sorry, I was thinking about lavender.' *Partly true*. 'What were you saying?'

His head tilted. 'Obviously nothing remotely

fascinating.' And then he grinned, gesturing left. 'I was asking you if you want to go down here?'

A quaint, narrow street, residential rather than commercial. Umbrella-free. Quieter.

He gave a little shrug. 'I was thinking it might take us to a vantage point over the valley.' His eyebrow cocked. 'I know how much you love a selfie with a view.'

Looking after her again, pandering to all her sweet spots. Making her heart hurt, making her smile. 'You know me so well.'

He struck out, chuckling. 'It's years of training.'

She caught him up. Years of training. Years of friendship.

Friendship...

That was all this was—warm feelings flying back and forth because they were friends. Had been for ever. So she had to stop fantasising, looking for meanings where there weren't any, reading desire into his eyes when it was only affection.

He was looking after her because she looked after him, listened to him when he needed an ear, advice, support. Hadn't he said as much before they came, that he wanted to even the balance sheet? And he'd bought her lavender because he was nice that way. Kind. He'd probably been thinking that, since the woman was engaging with them, she deserved to make a sale. And of course he *knew* that she would like it because she was into hand-tied bouquets and rustic arrangements. He was simply being his normal, sweet self and, if she wasn't careful, she was going to put a spoke in and ruin everything.

Enough!

Time to shift focus, talk about something safe.

She considered for a few seconds, then looked over. 'So anyway, how did it go with the read-through this morning? You never said…?'

'That's because there isn't much to say.' He shrugged. 'I mean, it went okay, but Caspar isn't in the early scenes. Scene one is just Saul and his mother, so Hayden and Trudi.'

'And how did Hayden do?' She pushed up her sunglasses so she could make eye contact, so he would see she was interested, see that, in spite of their afternoon jaunt, she hadn't forgotten the main mission. 'Did he read with conviction?'

Something flared briefly behind his gaze and then his jaw tightened.

'Of course he did. He is where he is today because he's a bloody good actor, and he's far too savvy to risk giving anything away until he absolutely has to. He'll keep stringing Franc along, giving *Darkness* one hundred percent, until he's got *Taurus* in the bag.' His mouth set firm. 'I think it's a bit low, actually.'

Steel in his gaze, uncharacteristic bile in his voice.

She felt something inside jarring, floundering.

Why was he looking at her like this? And why was he letting Hayden get to him all of a sudden? For sure, if Hayden was indeed stringing Franc along, then it wasn't great. But the movie industry was tricky, and they didn't know the whole story, so getting himself all wound up and judgemental was pointless—especially when he might benefit from the situation, when benefitting from the situation was exactly what he was hoping for.

She licked her lips, drawing in a careful breath. 'Maybe it seems that way, but who knows?' She loaded her gaze, trying to pull him back level. 'You might be faced with the same dilemma one day.'

His eyes flashed. 'Are you defending him?'

Her heart dipped. So much for levelling him out. 'No! I'm just saying that—'

He cut in, 'You like him, don't you?'

Thrown down hard like a gauntlet.

She felt her insides recoiling, then heat pulsing back, surging though her veins. 'What did you say?'

His gaze was locked on, burning, but then something was changing inside it, retreating a little. And then he was blinking, shrugging a bit. 'You spent a long time talking to him last night, so I just figured...'

Reddening ears, shifting on his feet. He was uncomfortable now; she could tell. Rightly so! Accusing her...*of what*? Fancying Hayden! Looking at her with that blistered gaze. Jumping down her throat. He might be toying with a white flag now, but she wasn't holding her peace. He deserved both barrels.

She slid her eyebrows up, feigning understanding. 'Oh, right. I can see how you would figure that…'

She raised her left hand, wriggling her fingers so he could see the ring. 'I'm engaged to *you*, sharing a room and a bed with *you*, so I can help *you* in your quest to be Saul, so *obviously* the first thing I'm going to do on our first night here is hit on Hayden Coulter in front of everybody as if I were single, as if I even *remotely* fancy the guy. Because *obviously* it makes total sense that I would want to shatter the illusion that— *oh, wait a minute*—I came here specifically to help *you* create.'

She widened her eyes at him. 'Great work, Sherlock! If the acting thing doesn't work out, there's always Special Branch!'

Borrowing the phrasing he'd used on her earlier; bemusement, of all things, surfacing in her eyes. She *was* cross, but there was an air of pantomime about it. Meanwhile, he was standing here in a pool of his own stupid jealousy, jealousy he shouldn't even be feeling, because she didn't belong to him.

Oh, God…

But he wanted her to, didn't he? *There!* He was admitting it. He was crushing on Jules big time—more than crushing—and he wanted to say it, let it out, because if ever there was a right moment, it was this one, since he was blown wide open anyway.

His heart clopped. But, if he let it out, then what? Because even though there had been that kaleidoscope in her eyes, looks that sometimes seemed to go deeper than affection, he couldn't be sure how deep, or what those looks really meant, or if he was even reading her right, because this was not their familiar landscape. This was new. Uncharted territory.

He swallowed. Besides, if he laid himself out and she didn't feel the same, then how would they carry on with this charade, sharing a room, a bed? Would she be lying there, wide awake in the darkness, wondering if he was thinking of trying it on?

He shuddered inside. He might have kissed her on impulse, but he would never... And she ought to know that because she knew *him*. But even so he *couldn't* put her in a situation where she might be worrying about it.

No.
No!
He couldn't go with the flow he'd inadvertently started, tell her the truth. It wouldn't set

him free. It would ruin everything. Which left only one option: smoke and mirrors...

He shifted stance, channelling every wise-cracking maverick he'd ever played, hating himself for it. 'Easy, tiger. I didn't say you were hitting on him. All I said was I got the impression you liked him.'

She blinked, seeming to replay the inciting conversation to herself. 'Oh.' And then a smile broke through thinly. 'Silly me. Must have been the way you said it...' Something flickered through her gaze. 'You sounded a bit miffed.'

Not letting it go. Going for the last word. But that was okay. He deserved it. He'd overreacted, lost control, but the thing was the fury wasn't going away. Rather, it was building, gathering like a storm, thundering between his temples. He could feel his blood beating, his skin prickling, guts struggling. Anger. Pain. Hurt. Layers piling up, pressing down, wanting to explode. Keeping his feelings for Jules inside was one thing, but he couldn't hold this in.

'Oh, I'm *more* than a bit miffed, Jules. I'm livid.'

She blanched. 'With me?'

His heart kinked. 'No! Of course not. It's Hayden! Franc.' White noise in his head. 'The whole situation.'

'Okay...' Her gaze settled, softening into his. 'Take a breath.'

He felt her warmth working its usual magic,
untangling his threads.

He inhaled, letting the words come. 'The thing
is, Franc is so decent—opening his home to us,
looking after us. He's investing in us. In *me*…'

Her eyes were holding him fast, making his
chest tighten, making his voice want to crack. 'He's
putting his faith in me, giving me a chance—*me*,
Jules. And there's Hayden, playing both sides…'
Abusing faith, trust, all the things worth having…
He forced himself to swallow. 'He's a fine actor.
I don't begrudge him his success but, now we're
getting to know Franc better, I can't help feeling
sick about what Hayden's doing, even if it *could*
work in my favour.'

'Oh, Alden.' She frowned and then her hand
was closing over his forearm, soft and warm. 'We
don't *know* for sure that he's *doing* anything.'
Her gaze was steady, a warm blue pool inviting
him in. 'I know what Joe told you, and I'm not
saying he isn't right, but he *could* be wrong. It's
all hearsay until it isn't, so working yourself up
like this is pointless.'

She shook her head a little. 'As for Franc, he
is decent, through and through, but I think the
reason you're feeling so protective of him has
got more to do with you than with him.' Her grip
tightened on his arm. 'You said it yourself just
now: he's put his faith in you, believes in you,
and it means the world. But it's making you hurt

too, isn't it, because those are the things you've always wanted from your parents.'

Her eyes were gleaming now, making his own burn, making his jaw want to tremble.

She could strip it down because she knew his pain: the guilt he lived with for not following the prescribed medical path. For wasting an expensive education on a flimsy, lightweight career that up until now had been exactly that. Lightweight movies, lightweight characters. He was living his parents' worst nightmare in glorious Technicolor, not only that, but living it with a reputation pinned to his back like tail on the bloody donkey!

She knew how he fought with himself every single day, all the fricking time: telling himself that he didn't need his parents' approval, telling himself that he was a grown up, responsible for his own choices, that what they thought didn't matter, but it did. *It did!* Always at the back of his mind, impelling him like thirst. Questing for approval, for the role that would finally make them sit up, pay attention, applaud him with warm, pleased smiles...

Her voice broke in, pulling him back.

'You're feeling hyper-loyal to Franc because he's giving you all the things your parents aren't, but also because you're a kind, sensitive person. You don't want to see him hurt or let down, and neither do I. But, you know, maybe he won't be.'

Her chin dipped. 'The thing to remember is that Franc is tough. He's seen terrible things in his life. He trekked to freedom carrying a sick mother on his own back—but he prevailed, and now he's at the top of his game. If Hayden bails, he isn't going to fall apart. It'll be an inconvenience, a fly in the ointment, but he *will* get past it...'

He felt her words soothing the turmoil out of him.

Of course...

Franc had been through hell, and because of that he hated conflict, but it didn't mean he couldn't handle adversity. It was *he,* Alden, who couldn't. Couldn't handle the thought of Jules liking Hayden, of Hayden shafting Franc. Two wires twisting into the wire that was already cutting into his flesh, the wire his parents had put there.

But he couldn't think any more about it now. Right now he needed to wind himself back in and show Jules some love, some appreciation, set them back on course.

He found a smile, aimed it at her. 'You're right. About everything. *As usual.*' The corners of her mouth curved up, and he felt released suddenly, a spark of wry humour returning. 'Franc's a tough guy. Meanwhile, I'm like one of those chicks that imprints on the poultry maid because the maid's the first thing it sees.'

She chuckled. 'I'm not sure Franc would enjoy *that* comparison.' And then the laughing light in her eyes was fading, giving way to seriousness. 'Can I say something about Hayden, just to finish?'

He felt his heart flinch but smiled on through. 'Of course.'

She released his arm and stepped back, meeting his gaze with a faint look of admonishment. 'If you'd bothered to ask me last night why I spent so much time talking to Hayden, I'd have told you the reason which is that I was *trying* to winkle something out of him about *Taurus*—unsuccessfully, before you ask.'

No guile in her eyes because when was there ever guile in Jules's eyes? Just the truth, shining. She'd been doing it for *him*, not because she liked Hayden or fancied him.

Not even remotely.

He felt a flicker of shame then warmth taking over, a new smile spreading into his cheeks. 'You tried, though, and I appreciate that.'

'Good.' She smiled, almost shyly, and suddenly he could feel more words rising.

'I appreciate you all the time, Jules…' She caught her bottom lip between her teeth, blinking the way she did when she was trying to rein in her emotions, but he wasn't in the mood for stopping. He needed to say this.

'I appreciate you for coming, for being here—for being my friend all these years.' Her eyes were glistening now, making his own throat burn, putting a crack in his voice. 'For talking me off the stupid ledges I get myself onto. For putting up with me—'

'Stop it!' Her throat was working. 'Stop right now, do you hear?' She wiped her eyes and then her gaze locked onto his, kaleidoscope swirling. 'I don't *mind* putting up with you! It's not *even* putting up with you!' She was shaking her head now. 'It's not like that with us. Ever. Okay?'

He felt his heart giving and then the urge was coming, same as in the woods, turning itself into words, tumbling out before he could stop them. 'Come here, you…' He opened his arms, heart drumming. 'Please?'

Her gaze widened into his, searching, and then she was coming forwards, melting in. He felt her arms tightening around his back, his breath slowing, time slowing. It felt so right, holding her like this, being held. Breathing her in, feeling her body close and warm, and maybe she was feeling it too because she wasn't moving.

But then all too soon she was, shifting, detaching herself, stepping back a little, her eyes still wet but glowing.

'Just so you know, you don't have to ask me every time.'

CHAPTER FOURTEEN

SHE LIFTED HIS tee-shirt off the chair, toying with it. Did she dare?

She felt a flutter, a small squirm of guilt starting, but the tug of the tee-shirt was too strong. She pressed it to her face, breathing in.

It smelt clean, line-dried, even though he'd been wearing it yesterday, knocking about on the tennis court with Jason Lewis, sweating. But then Alden always had a clean smell about him. After squash, at school. After running. After gym. Always fresh. Wholesome. Not perfumed, though. He didn't go in for cologne. In the bathroom, just his shaving foam, razor, soap. Toothbrush.

She nosed the cotton again. He'd be weirded out if he could see her, or maybe he'd laugh. But he wasn't here. He was downstairs, hopefully reading the hell out of Caspar, now that they'd got to his scenes. And she was supposed to be going for a swim, but then she'd noticed his tee-shirt. *Enough!*

She put it back, adjusting it so it looked undisturbed, then she picked up her things and went down.

Outside the air felt thick. Hot. Even on the shaded parts of the path she could feel its pulse beating on her skin. Or maybe her skin was beating because of the tee-shirt. Thinking about it. His lovely scent. That warm, enveloping whoosh of it every time they hugged which, since Grasse, they were doing more and more…

Such as yesterday, when the strap of her flip-flop had snapped as they were going up the steps from the tennis court. She'd pitched forward, thinking she was a goner, but he'd caught her, all concerned: *'Are you okay?'* And then he'd been pulling her in close, hugging the shock out of her, his body warm and firm, stirring a little weakness inside, a little fire.

But it wasn't only hugging. They were touching more too—not just in front of the others, because they were 'engaged', but also when they were alone. Little touches, brief. His hand coming to her arm or her shoulder when they were walking. His head coming close when they were laughing, so close that she could feel his hair skimming hers.

And every time it happened, she could feel that electric thrill tingling, that illicit tug starting, stirring the old awareness back to vibrant life, making her want something she shouldn't want, wanting it so badly that now she was going around sniffing his tee-shirts!

She shifted the tote on her shoulder, feeling the wetness evaporating where the strap had been. So hot! A throbbing, bounding kind of heat. She licked her lips. Maybe it was sunstroke, summer madness that was bending her brain, fuelling her fantasies about Alden. Or maybe the touching was to blame, the newness of it…

She felt a frown coming. Weird how they'd never really touched. It wasn't as if Alden was closed off, more the opposite, and she definitely wasn't. She hugged her other friends all the time. But somehow, with Alden, it was as if she'd stayed trapped inside that teenage moment on his bed, waiting for another nudge of his foot, or some other touch that never came.

And because it had never come, she hadn't felt bold enough to breach the barrier in case it messed up their friendship, and he'd never seemed inclined to, except when she was upset—crying—and then, oh, then he was warm, and kind, and gentle, holding her, looking after her, doing everything right, treating her like a princess.

As he was doing now. Increasingly.

She mounted the steps that cut through the high boundary hedge and paused, scanning the pool, the curve of its sides and the weathered flagstones, scanning but not really seeing.

Probably it was because they were together more. Probably some of the faking was bleeding into real life. And of course she'd opened things up the other day, hadn't she? Saying that if he wanted to hug her, he didn't have to ask first.

She crossed into the shade, dropping her tote onto a lounger, sinking down next to it.

All the time now, little touches, warm hugs. Before, only ever putting his arms around her when she was distraught because distress was, what? She felt a tingle. An acceptable reason for contact? An excuse? As if without an *acceptable* reason, without an *excuse*, he didn't feel able to…

She felt her mouth opening, stiffening.

Those times on his bed. His foot. Her foot. Had he been waiting for *her,* waiting for her to nudge him back, look at him, give him a sign? Her heart pulsed. All this time, had he been waiting for permission? Her heart pulsed again, double-time. Did he like her—like her in *that* way? The way she liked him? Had he always…? Never dared… Never thought…

Oh, God! Could it be?

She pressed her lips together, rubbing them with her finger. It certainly explained what had reared up out of him on that street in Grasse. That jealous edge on his voice over Hayden. The way he'd come over to plant a possessive hand on her waist when she'd been talking to Hayden that first night.

She'd told herself it was for show, a fiancé staking his claim to look the part, but on that street there'd been no one to show. Just that affronted edge on his voice that had played to her heart like hurt, hurt she couldn't bear to hear because it was so utterly unfounded.

It was why she had launched herself back at him so hard, exposing herself without even thinking, because she couldn't believe he could imagine that she would ever be interested in Hayden Coulter when it was him…

Him.

She swallowed hard. Since for ever. From the beginning. Always him. That little leap inside every time his eyes found hers; that flutter starting when he came through the door, smiling. That magic that had always seemed to twinkle between them. That lightness, that ease. Soul mate stuff ramped to the max now because they were together so much, sharing a secret, a room, a bed; hugs, laughter…everything.

She closed her eyes. It was why she missed him like crazy when he wasn't here; why she was missing him right now. Craving his smile, his energy, the sweet sight of him. The scent of his damn tee-shirt! Being here together like this was breaking down the barriers, letting the light in, revealing all the truths. *The* truth…

I love him.

Her breath stilled. In love with her best friend,

the one she couldn't live without, the one she couldn't afford to lose, the one whose voice she always wanted to hear whatever time of the day or night it was.

And Sam *had* known. She felt hot tears welling. Of course he bloody well had.

'*What am I for, Jules?*'

Except it had really been, *what am* I *for? Now* she could hear it, that inflexion she'd missed, or maybe she'd just blinded herself to it, along with the truth, because she didn't know what to do with the truth.

She sat for a moment, then pulled out her towel, wiped her face. And now what? Should she let it out, tell Alden?

Her stomach clenched. No. She couldn't. Not here. Not now. Because what if she was wrong, misreading everything? Misreading the hugging and the touching and the sweet light in his eyes because of the heat, the situation? For sure he *had* sounded jealous over Hayden that day in Grasse, but he'd also been steamed up about Hayden, and about Franc, and about his own parents. His reaction to her 'defending' Hayden could have been bound up in all that. And that tight hand on her waist the first night could have been exactly what she'd thought at the time—just Alden acting the part of a possessive fiancé. As for that kiss, she still wasn't sure about that…

She sucked at her lip. Bottom line, she wasn't

sure about anything, except that coming clean could ruin everything and, thanks to Mum, she knew what ruin felt like. She couldn't go there again, especially not with Alden.

Not with him.

So, that left, what?

She drew in a long, slow breath to clear her head. That left waiting. Maybe until he got back from Cairo, which was where he was heading the moment they got back. Ten days in the desert, playing a baddie for a change. She smiled inside. He was stoked.

She got up, rooting in her bag for her book, hat, sunscreen. Waiting felt right. She could wait. What difference would it make after all this time? And, yes, he could fall for one of his co-stars in Egypt, but if that happened then she was clearly on the wrong beat anyway!

She stripped off her sarong, dropping it onto the lounger. In the meantime, she would keep her head, tune in, assess things. It was the only way. She couldn't afford a fatal blunder, risk—

'Jules?'

Alden!

She spun round, almost colliding with him as he came to a skidding halt in front of her. For the briefest moment, his eyes flicked downward, but then they were back, burning into hers.

'It's happening, Jules. *Happened!* Hayden's quitting!'

'What?' She felt her heart stopping and firing up again. 'When? How?'

'A short while ago. He left the room to take a call and then he came back in, asked Franc if he could have a word…' His eyes widened, flashing blue. 'It was all over his face! The others thought there was a tragedy in his family but I…' He pressed a hand to his head. 'Anyway, then Franc came back in and told us.'

'How did he seem?' Because in spite of everything she'd said about Franc's resilience, it was impossible not to feel for him.

Alden shrugged. 'Subdued. But calm. We're picking up with the session tomorrow.' His eyebrows lifted. 'Like you said, he's tough, carrying on regardless.'

'That's good.'

She felt her pulse steadying. Not abandoning the read-through could only work in Alden's favour, give him the chance to impress, start pitching for the Saul part. It was clearly already on his mind, moving behind his gaze along with that scrawl of self-doubt his parents could wipe away in a heartbeat if only…

But they weren't going to, not any time soon. So it was for her to see him through this, keep him right. Thank goodness they'd pushed through that barrier of not touching, because right now she wanted to touch him, wanted him to feel her love, even if she couldn't say it out loud.

She took hold of his shoulders, loading her gaze. 'And how are you feeling?'

He puffed out his cheeks. 'Relieved, mostly. Now whatever happens, at least I'm not carrying it around with me.' And then his gaze softened, tightening on hers. 'The other thing I'm feeling is grateful…' Depths in his eyes, tugging at her, turning her inside out. 'For you.' He shook his head a little. 'I'm so glad you're here, Jules. If you weren't, who would I tell?'

She licked her lips trying not to look at his, trying not to notice the warmth of his shoulders in her hands or his nearness, her own near nakedness. 'Still me. Except I'd be on the end of the phone, probably up a ladder festooned in ivy or something, but I'd be here for you one way or the other.' She tilted her head, going for what she hoped would emerge as a best-friend smile. 'You *know* that.'

'Always here for me.' A smile touched his lips and then suddenly his arms were going around her, pulling her in, and it was warm soft cotton against her skin, hard muscle rippling underneath, and that clean, lovely smell of him.

She closed her eyes, luxuriating. If he'd arrived one minute earlier, she'd still have been wearing her sarong. But now it was just her bikini, and his body, the divine sensations of skin and fabric, muscle, and warmth. Impossible not to fold, melt in, cling to him, to the moment, imagining…

But no. *No!* She couldn't spiral out. This was precisely the kind of confusion she didn't need. This was a hug. Nothing more. He was hugging her because she was here for him and he was grateful, because the thing he'd been churning himself up about for days had finally happened and he was feeling released, excited, anxious.

She swallowed hard, making to disengage, and he let go of her instantly, stepping aside with a smile.

She smiled back. Just a hug, definitely. The thing to do was to move on quickly, keep the conversation going as if she hadn't just been thinking all the things she'd been thinking.

'So…' She bent to pick up her sarong, tying it around herself as nonchalantly as she could, taking her time so she could use the moment to gather herself. 'What's the plan now?'

Plan A would be to stop allowing his gaze to slide south of her collar bones, but he was only human, and the temptation to look was overpowering. Hard enough at school when the girls had been condemned to those regulation high-necked one-pieces. All he'd got in those days was that Jules had legs up to here. The rest had been down to his imagination.

But he didn't need to imagine now. Curves he'd never seen unclothed before, let alone felt crushed against him, were in the process of being swathed in that spoilsport sarong.

He drew in a breath. Probably it was for the best. Holding her practically naked had nearly done for him. Holding tight, clenching his teeth, knowing that at any second his traitorous body could give him away. Christ, even thinking about it now was turning him on. Her breasts pressing into him. Her bright heat. The silky caress of her hair, the smell of her skin.

Years of not touching, not hugging, and now it was happening all the time. Flowing together, feeling so right, like second nature. But was she feeling the same things as him? The tingling undertow, the shifting air pressure? Or was it just him quivering inside because he was sliding backwards in his heart, wanting her more with every little touch, every hug, every beat of his pulse?

Head bent, hair blowing, hands busy knotting the sheer fabric…

Why couldn't he read her? He'd always been able to, or thought so, but now… He swallowed hard. Too immersed. Too close to see the bigger picture. Struggling to separate fantasy from reality. That was his pattern, wasn't it? Because he was suggestible. *Hopeful*. Prone to fantasising, falling. Prone to messing up. Just four days with his best friend and here he was, tumbling down the same old rabbit hole, thrilling inside whenever her eyes caught his, feeling his breath catching every time she smiled.

And the touching was complicating things, tangling all his strings so that he couldn't tell left from right, and now she was asking him about a plan, as if he could even think straight!

He pressed a finger to his eyelid. But it was an obvious question. Sensible. Logical. If wanted to make that leap from Caspar to Saul, then he needed a plan. A strategy. He needed to put that centre, not let himself get distracted, because in two days they were leaving, and the second he touched down he'd be off again, to Cairo. Two days to secure the lead role. But how?

He moistened his lips, meeting Jules's lifting gaze. 'I haven't got a plan. But I need one. Should I strike while the iron's hot or wait?'

Her brow pleated. 'Somewhere in the middle.' She dropped down onto the lounger. 'I mean, Franc needs to take it in, doesn't he? And I don't know how these things work, but I guess he'll need to talk to the producers…'

His heart seized. How could he have forgotten about the producers, the executives, the money people?

'You're right.' He pushed a hand through his hair, feeling the wind dying in his sails, his thirty-seconds-old resolve to strategise his way into the Saul part fizzling away.

'He's probably on the phone to them right now.

Hayden's a big box-office draw so I imagine they'll be having a little freak out.' He could feel bitterness trickling in, shaping his voice into an exaggerated upbeat tone. 'But hey, never mind, Alden Phillips is happy to step in, take up the slack…'

Jules looked at him, her lips parting slightly as if he was speaking a foreign language, but he was on a roll now, couldn't curb the impulse to splash about in it.

He bent his voice the other way, assuming a gravelly, mid-Atlantic producer's voice. 'Alden *who*? Oh, *that* guy! The one who was dating Natasha Forbes and Justine Black and Chloe Symmons and—'

'Just loving that attitude, pal!' Jules lifted her hands up, slow-clapping. 'You're going to walk right into the part toting that bag of insecurities!'

He swallowed down the last drops of bitterness and shrugged. 'Even if I leave it at the door, you know what I'm saying is true.' He sat down beside her, but not too close. 'I want that part—know I can do it—but I don't have the currency.'

'How can you say that?' She drew one leg up, angling herself towards him. 'You're hardly a nobody. You make movies. Audiences love you.'

He felt clarity arriving. 'Jules, they love me for precisely the reason the producers won't want me—I act in one dimension. I save damsels in distress, deliver pithy one-liners.'

'But you deliver them well. Everything you do, you do well. And Franc wouldn't have cast you at all if he thought you were one-dimensional. He cast you because he can see your potential.' Her eyes were filling with that magnetic, bolstering gleam. 'Franc's a kingmaker, and I think he's for the underdog because he was one himself once. I think if you can *show* him Saul, and he likes what he sees, then he'll knock down the doubters like skittles.'

He felt the words settling, making sense.

She was right. *Of course* she was right! Meanwhile he was so steeped in his own insecurity that he was losing his own plot.

He broke away from her gaze, staring at the pool, letting the turquoise water blur into glinting spangles. Why was he always so quick to throw himself under the wheels instead of hitching himself to the onward-rolling wagon? Franc *was* for the underdog. The fact that he, Alden Phillips, was here was proof enough of that.

And for sure, Hayden was box-office gold, but how many films had Franc made that had turned lesser actors *into* that same box-office gold? For God's sake, it was exactly why he'd asked Jacklyn to get him an audition in the first place. Franc wasn't just an inspirational director—a kind, thoroughly decent human being—but he was also a conduit. And somehow he'd forgotten that, lost it under all these other layers, all of them called Juliana Beckett…

His heart dipped, then filled. Jules had his back, his front, his every which way, but he *had* to get his head straight, find his focus, and how could he do that when she was stealing it all the time? Even now, he could feel awareness tugging, his fingers itching to lace themselves into hers, drawing out her smile and all that lovely light in her eyes.

He blinked, bringing the pool back into focus. When he'd come down here looking for her, he'd been going to propose an outing because that was what he'd promised her, but maybe what he really needed was space. Alone time. Just for a while.

He turned to look at her and instantly her eyes lit. 'So, have you given yourself a good talking to?'

In spite of himself, he felt a smile coming. 'I have. My conclusions are that you are right, and that I'm an idiot. I've got nothing to lose with Franc. I just need to pick my moment and be confident about it.' He mimed a deep bow, doffing an imaginary hat, because hugging her would only set his strings jumping again. 'Thank you. I don't know how you do it, but you always put me right.'

She split a grin. 'Hey, I'm your friend: that's my job.' And then she blew out a breath. 'So, what's the plan?'

That question again, but now at least he had an answer.

He tightened his gaze on hers, hoping she wouldn't read rejection in it. 'I'm going to go for a run, to settle, you know, and then I really need to start learning my lines for next week.'

'Oh…' She blinked, surprised perhaps, but she didn't seem hurt, which was a relief. And then her hand touched his back just for second. 'I think a run will do you good.' She smiled. 'Just don't get sunstroke!'

CHAPTER FIFTEEN

SHE PAUSED TO savour the air. Jasmine. Damp grass.
The faintest tang of the sea. She rolled her head
from side to side, feeling her shoulders loosening,
the tension inside relenting a little. Being outside
in the dawn with Franc's secateurs in her hand was
so much better than lying awake, trying not to toss
and turn, trying not to disturb Alden.

She stepped into the border, minding her feet,
cutting random stems of ornamental grasses, liking their frothy fronds, and then she straightened,
considering the Euphorbia. Imposing. Sculptural.
But the sap was an irritant and she didn't have
gloves.

She laid her grasses in the trug and moved
on. Probably, though, it would be hard to disturb
Alden once he was asleep. Out. For. The. Count.
Must be all that thinking and overthinking he
did, wearing him out. The rhythm of his breathing hadn't changed at all as she'd slipped out of
the bed and got dressed. Yesterday's shorts. *His*
discarded tee-shirt because it smelt of him. It was

the kind of thing a real fiancée would do and, anyway, he'd never know. She would be back and changed before he woke.

She set the trug down, leaning in to cut some stems of bold rudbeckia. Must be nice, being able to switch off like Alden could, dropping into sleep like a stone into water. She couldn't, not when her head was whirling. It was why she was here, up and about. Whirring away. Wondering. Churning.

All very well resolving to wait, to see if she could tell what he was feeling, *if* he was feeling for her what she was feeling for him, but now that Hayden had actually quit, left the building, he was like a cat on a hot tin roof, wanting her support but seeming not to want her company.

He hadn't said it in words, but it had been there in his eyes yesterday. Distance creeping in. Taking himself off for a run to *settle*, then cloistering himself on the balcony with next week's script, so quiet at dinner that he might as well not have been there, although maybe the same could have been said for everyone around that table.

Whatever! She got it. Hayden leaving *was* a big deal. Of course Alden needed some thinking space, and he *did* have a job to do next week; *did* have lines to learn. It all stacked up, made sense, except…

She felt her heart constricting, tears prickling. Except she couldn't stop herself from feeling a

little bit crushed, a little bit rejected. *Mum's fault!*
Because of Mum, she couldn't handle the feeling
of being pushed away, shut out, brushed off. Not
by people who mattered. She was overly sensitive, primed like a fuse, but knowing it didn't
stop the feelings coming—rising, boiling, churning her up inside. Helplessness. Worthlessness.
Loneliness. Jabbing. Poking. Stinging. Hurting
all the more because it was Alden triggering the
mother lode: the one she loved; the one she'd always loved…

She laid the rudbeckia down and wiped her
face, breathing deeply to calm herself. Ridiculous, getting this overwrought. He absolutely
wasn't trying to hurt her. She knew that. She
was just too hooked on hope, too high on wanting, longing. The higher the climb, the harder
the fall! Wasn't this exactly why she'd resolved
to step back? To wait. Watch!

She picked up the trug and walked on. The
problem was, how to watch when he wasn't
around to be watched? Was that the writing on
the wall right there? If he could switch lanes so
easily, hold himself away from her in a heartbeat, then maybe…

She glanced at her hand. Wearing his ring, but
she wasn't his. Just here to help him achieve his
dream. That was why he'd asked her. Oh, he'd
plated it up nicely, promising fun and sunshine—
which he *was* delivering—but, bottom line, he

was bent on his career. Always had been. So determined that, even though his parents weren't on side, even though it cost him every day that they weren't in his camp, he wouldn't give it up. He was laser-focused, stronger than he knew.

She felt her breath settling. And wasn't that, in truth, one of the things she loved about him—the way he was always feeling the fear but doing it anyway, making his way, slowly but surely, up that greasy pole? God, all the fears and insecurities they'd shared through the years, taking them to heart for each other, so that his struggles were hers, and hers were his. And now he was on the cusp, teetering. Of course he was jangling, preoccupied! *Of course.* He wouldn't *be* Alden Phillips if he wasn't!

She let out a breath, letting her gaze drift along the border. Which brought her full circle, none the wiser. She felt the secateurs in her hand. At least there was this: Franc's lovely garden. The gentle warmth of the sun. A bit of breeze stirring fragrance about. This was peaceful. Soothing.

She bent to clip some lavender stems but then a figure caught her eye, rounding the end of the border, softly dressed for yoga, or meditation perhaps.

Franc!

She felt a flick of self-consciousness. He'd given her the run of his garden, but he probably hadn't expected to encounter her at this time of the morning. And there was nowhere to hide. Too late, anyway. He'd seen her, was coming nearer, approaching, breaking into a smile.

'Good morning.' Light-green eyes held her, warm, flecked with amber. 'You're up early.'

She felt her awkwardness leaving, a smile arriving. 'I wasn't sleeping so thought I'd take you up on your offer to have a poke about in the garden.'

'Ah.' His eyes darted to the trug. 'I look forward to seeing what you do with your haul.'

'It's hardly a haul. Not yet anyway.' She tucked her hair behind her ear to fill the pause. 'You look as if you have meditation in mind.'

He cast a glance at his clothes. 'That was the plan, but I'm not in a hurry.' And then his head tilted. 'Why weren't you sleeping, Jules?'

His gaze was gentle, searching.

She felt a white lie rising, something about being too warm, or thirsty, but no. She didn't want to lie to Franc. But what to say? And maybe he was reading her mind because suddenly he went on, throwing out a suggestion.

'I hope it isn't because of what happened yesterday…?' His eyebrows lifted. 'Because Alden mustn't be worried about the film, and you mustn't be worrying yourself on his behalf.' He motioned to a bench a few yards back. 'Shall we sit for a moment?'

She felt a tingle. If Franc wanted to talk about

Alden, then maybe she could turn the conversation in Alden's favour somehow, help him get the Saul part.

She nodded, smiled. 'Sure.'

On the bench, Franc settled back, crossing one leg over the other. 'I could see Alden was troubled at dinner last night. I mean, we were all subdued, but he must relax. The film itself isn't in jeopardy.' He paused for a long moment and then a smile touched his lips. 'I know it means a lot to him— not only because it's his favourite book, but because…' He was circling his hand, searching for the right words, clearly trying to be diplomatic.

Her belly pulsed. She could just say it—spare him.

'Because it's a *good* role, the kind of role he's been desperate to do.' She levelled her gaze at him. 'In a nutshell, it's a game-changer.'

Franc registered the words, acknowledging, and the acknowledgement felt like prompt, or maybe she was just looking for an excuse to say more, to fill him in, so he'd know where Alden was coming from.

'He only got into doing the movies he's known for because they were the ones he was offered. And now they keep offering him more of the same—and he's grateful, because he wants to work, but he's typecast. And it's frustrating for him because he wants to be stretched, show more of what he can do…'

Franc's eyes flickered with a faint bemusement, but she didn't care. She was on a roll now,
voicing Alden's thoughts, feeling his passion running through her and she wasn't stopping until
she'd said everything. 'He's sick of playing one-
dimensional characters. He wants to be taken
seriously. He isn't up himself or anything. He
just loves film as a medium—the power of it,
the beauty...'

And then his darkened room was coming back,
his boy's body next to her on the bed pushing
out heat, light from the screen bathing his lovely
face. She felt a smile curving on her lips. 'He's
into the great directors, and the niche ones, the
arty ones, and the ones who push boundaries,
like you. He loves acting, always has, but it's
bigger than that with him. He *feels* film, bleeds
it. He's besotted with cinema.'

Franc's chin lifted on a smile. 'And with you,
clearly.'

Her heart squeezed. Was it Alden's devoted-
fiancé performance that was convincing Franc
or...?

She pushed the thought away, flashing her
ring finger, going for humour. 'I should jolly
well hope so.'

He chuckled and then his expression settled.
'Anyway, I really just wanted to say that you can
sleep easy—Alden too. We'll get through this.'

She smiled. Getting through was fine, but it

wasn't getting her where she wanted to be. She needed to tilt the sail, push Alden right under Franc's nose.

She licked her lips, mustering a sympathetic look. 'All the same, losing Hayden must be a blow.'

His shoulders lifted. 'It's the way it goes sometimes.'

Go on, Jules...

'Do you have a replacement in mind?'

His eyes lifted, as if he was trying to read his own forehead. 'We screen-tested a few. I'll have to go back, reconsider—'

'Or...' She could feel her stomach clenching, her mouth drying. 'You could try Alden in the part?'

His gaze lowered to hers. 'Alden.'

She swallowed past the dryness, trying to keep her voice even and business-like. 'He knows it off by heart, Franc, knows the character inside out. He could bring a lot to the role.' She licked her bottom lip, clinging tightly to her nerve. 'Not saying he isn't thrilled to be Caspar, because he is, truly. I'm only thinking out loud here, thinking what harm could it do to give him a try?'

Franc stared at her for a long, nerve-wracking second and then his gaze was softening, lengthening, weighing it up. 'None, I suppose, not if he wanted to...'

Alden drew up, scanning the swathe of well-mown grass in front of him. If Jules had come this way, heading for the woods, she'd have disturbed the dew, left a trail of footprints. But the grass was pristine, as it had been on every other side of the house.

He blew out a breath and turned round. He'd have put money on her going for a walk in the woods but clearly he was out of touch. He ground his jaw. Out of touch, out of reach! He'd pulled back to create some space in his head—a *Jules-free* zone—so he could focus on how he was going to tackle Franc about the Saul part, but it hadn't worked. *Wasn't* working…

He struck out for the south-facing garden. Keeping Jules at arm's length was only messing with his head more, taking up all the room inside it, because they didn't *do* distance. Not deliberately. She had her life—her business and her other friends. *Boyfriends!* And he had his life— on the go, littered with ups and downs, usually because of women. But through it all they had always had each other, and through it all, when it came to his career, he'd always been able to hold his focus. But now…?

His heart thumped. Now, everything was different. Everything was Jules. And he'd thought it was because he was too close to see, thought that if he stepped back, he'd find some perspective, but all he'd found was a bigger screen, Jules filling it side to side. Filling it with the hurt she was trying to hide because he wasn't talking to her as he usually did, filling it with her sweet, brave smile and her plucky, 'I understand' voice.

And then he'd come to, surfacing out of a dream on her side of the bed. Breathing in her pillow smell, hand searching for her because the bliss was still playing at the edges of his consciousness— her mouth kissing him, her hands trailing down his back—and he didn't want it to end. He'd been rock-hard, muzzy-headed, aching for her, but she was gone.

So he'd got up. And he didn't know what to do with all these feelings, how to broach them with her, *if* he even should broach them, but what he did know was that he needed to find her, be himself with her again, because distance was not a solution.

Across the breakfast terrace, down the steps, gravel crunching, more grass, roses, insects humming, voices burbling—

Voices!

He stopped to listen, trying to gauge the direction, then turned right through a rose arch, following the sound, following a narrow grassy path that bordered a dense sheltering hedge.

With every step he could feel excitement mounting, tingling. Definitely Jules! He'd know the rise and fall of her voice anywhere. He quickened his pace, resisting the urge to run, because how lame would that look? On the other hand, he didn't want her to think he was just happening by. He wanted her to know he was looking for her, that he was sorry for being distant.

And then the hedge was running out, giving way to the butt end of a deep herbaceous border. He tailed around it and his heart vaulted.

Jules!

Sitting on a bench a short distance away, trug at her feet, one leg pulled up under her, talking to Franc. Franc was in loose pants and a top: *yoga gear.* Jules was in shorts and—he blinked— *his* navy V-neck, the tee-shirt he'd left on the chair last night, the one he'd been going to grab but couldn't find. *On her...* On the big side, but somehow...

He felt his lips trying to twitch, a small, inexplicable thrill of happiness rising but he didn't have long to savour it because suddenly her eyes were lifting, as if she'd felt him there, and then a smile was breaking over her lovely face, a warm, full smile.

'Good morning, sleepy head.'

'Good morning.' He was definitely thinking the words, but perhaps they never emerged, because suddenly there were a hundred sensations milling and swirling: his feet moving, somehow carrying him to the bench; his hand wrapping around hers, her fingers squeezing back; her eyes coming to his, forgiveness and warmth inside them. Bending, which felt like tumbling, to kiss the top of her head, the fragrant softness of her hair against his lips, feeling—*how?*—that she was closing her eyes, melting a little, or maybe it was just the sigh of her breath.

And then Franc's voice broke in as if everything in the world was normal. 'Your ears must have been burning, Alden!'

'Oh?' He glanced at Jules; got the confirmation he was looking for. They'd been talking about him. He straightened, aiming a smile at Franc. 'In a good way, I hope.'

'Of course.' Franc's eyes crinkled. 'Jules has been singing your praises to the heavens, convincing me that I should be looking at you as a possibility for Saul...'

The words took a moment to register.

'Me?'

'Just a test, if you want to?'

He could feel Jules's fingers gripping his, squeezing frantically, urging him to say something, but he was too busy reeling to speak.

All this time, wrestling with how to bring this exact thing about, burrowing into the shell of himself, thinking he needed space, distance *to think*. And Jules had, what, just bumped into Franc at dawn, trug in hand, casually cutting her flowers, putting his case *at the same time*?

He felt a smile coming then leaving again. It should have been him, putting his own case, but he'd been too busy overthinking it, hadn't he? Tangling himself up about it, and why?

A wave of bitterness roiled in his stomach. Not because of the part. Oh, he wanted it all right, for itself; of course he did. But mostly, *mostly*, for what it could bring: not awards and accolades but a nod from his parents, some token acknowledgement that he was doing all right, that the choice he'd made was every bit as valid as theirs.

Years dragging this weight around, that he was somehow a disappointment, and now here was Jules trying to help, trying to heft him over the hurdle of himself, squeezing his hand so hard she was cutting off his circulation.

He pulled in a breath. *Enough!* It was time to drop the weight and rise. Jules was on his side and that was all that mattered.

He drew Franc back into focus. 'Oh, I want to.' Jules's fingers dug in, crushing his harder. 'I mean, a lot. Very much.'

'Good.' Franc smiled and then he was getting to his feet. 'Stay behind after the read-through today and show me what you've got.' He gave a little shrug. 'As you know, casting isn't entirely up to me, but we'll see…'

'I understand.'

Franc made to go, then stopped. 'Whatever happens with the part, Alden, you're going to be all right.' His eyes darted to Jules and came back smiling. 'You're marrying your biggest fan!' And then he was turning, walking away, throwing up a hand. 'See you both at breakfast!'

He felt the blood beating in his temples, rever-
berating into the chasm where thoughts should
have been.

He looked at Jules. 'Did that just happen? Is
he really giving me a try?'

She scrunched her face up. 'I think "show me
what you've got" is reasonably definitive.' And
then suddenly she was extricating her hand from
his. 'FYI, before you get any ideas, I'm *not* that
big a fan. I was just laying it on thick for Franc.'

Cutting straight to humour, skipping the apology scene. He could let it go, but then it would
only weigh on him, and he was sick of weight.
This was Jules. He *had* to put things right.

He sat down next to her, pulling her hand back
into his. 'I see you, Jules—know what you're trying to do—but please, before I fall at your feet
to worship you for what you just did, I want to
say sorry for what *I* did, going off like that, with-
drawing, being distant.'

Silence. And then her lips pressed together.
'You needed space.'

Brave words, but tears were welling at the
edges of her eyes.

He felt his heart twisting. If only he could tell
her she was the cause, the effect, at the heart of
everything. But he couldn't risk a spanner in the
works, not now when he didn't know what she'd
say back, when he needed not to be distracted

and churning, when he needed to be laser-focused on the opportunity that she'd secured for him.

He squeezed her hand, loading his gaze. 'I *thought* I needed space. Turns out I didn't know what I needed, so I'm sorry if you were hurt.' *Take responsibility, Alden!* 'What I mean is, I'm sorry for hurting you. I didn't mean to. I'd never…'

A familiar glimmer was surfacing in her gaze, drawing him on, drawing more words out. 'I'm an idiot, okay?' Her eyes registered agreement, triggering a smile inside. He let a little of it out, just a touch. 'You're perfect, by the way.'

She sucked her lips to one side, holding his gaze, and then suddenly a smile was breaking her face apart, lighting up her eyes. 'You're right. I *am* perfect.' And then her chin dipped. 'And, so you know, it was actually all right without you. Peaceful.'

He felt his heart filling, bursting, showering warmth. 'There you go again.'

'What?'

'Being cute. Letting me off the hook.'

Her eyebrows went up. 'Well, what would you have me to do, *darling*?' She pressed her free hand to her chest, fluttering her lids. 'Tell you that I *missed* you, that I didn't know what to *do* without you? That I was *miserable* every second because you were learning your *lines* instead of trying to persuade me that tennis is a fun game?'

And then her hand dropped back to her lap, and she was Jules again, leaning in, eyeballing him. 'You know where that road goes, don't you…?'

She was playing with him now, enjoying herself.

He felt a fresh smile twitching. 'Go on. I can see you've got a good one.'

She laughed. 'That road goes right back to me being your biggest fan, and as I said before, I'm not that big a fan, only moderately enamoured.'

Laughing at her own cleverness, but that was fine because he could feel a diamond of his own taking shape, a gift, really.

He licked his top lip, fastening his eyes on hers. 'Only *moderately* enamoured?'

She stopped laughing and then her eyes were narrowing, giving him the suspicious side-eye.

He could feel his belly vibrating, the coveted last word jumping for joy on his tongue. He let go of her hand, tugging a section of navy-blue hem. 'In that case, why are you wearing my tee-shirt?'

CHAPTER SIXTEEN

ALDEN WAS SQUINTING at his phone, turning it this way and that, trying to orientate the map. 'I think the marina's this way…'

'You're right.' She held in a smile. 'According to the sign, anyway.'

'What sign?' His head whipped round, following her gaze to the sign he was standing under, and then his eyes came back to hers, full of withering, smiling light. 'Very clever, Miss Clever Clogs.'

'It's not cleverness, just simple observation.'

'Humph!' He pocketed his phone and then he was motioning for her to walk, a wry smile hanging on his lips. 'Come on, eagle eye.'

'Bleary eye, more like.'

'Are you complaining?'

Her heart gave. 'No, of course not.' Although, after the late night they'd had going over and over his audition with Franc—how well it had gone—feeling his hand shaking her awake at five a.m. *had* come as a shock.

Last day, he'd said. Last chance to take her out,

since he was going to be tied up from late morning onwards finishing the script read-through with Franc and the others. And hadn't he promised her Saint Tropez? They could go there for breakfast. Alain Delon, Brigitte Bardot, remember...?

Alden...

Driving along the coast with the top down, his Saint Tropez playlist blasting, singing along with *Come Fly with Me*. And then it had been parking in a leafy square, staring blankly at the ticket machine until a friendly local had come the rescue, showing them which buttons to press in which order.

And now they were marina-bound, strolling along a narrow pastel street with shop shutters rattling up, displays being set out.

Balmy air.

Pink-gold light.

And *him*.

She flicked him a glance. Navy chino crops hanging low on his hips. Blue-and white-striped shirt. Fresh-looking. Sun-kissed. *Gorgeous!*

She felt a low-down tug, an ache starting. Aching all the time. Fluttering. She couldn't stop it happening, couldn't stop remembering that look on his face when he'd found her with Franc yesterday: joy, warmth, and something else that had set her heart leaping. And then he'd been coming over, his eyes full of apology, wrapping his hand around hers, kissing her head, stealing her breath with the sheer power of it.

And she would have accepted that silent sorry, left it there, but after Franc had gone, instead of falling straight into his own happiness, he'd apologised again, eyes reaching in so far that for a moment she'd thought she was going to come undone, tell him everything. But she'd bottled it, flicked on the safety, opting for humour. And then everything had slotted back in nice and snug, as if none of the rest had happened at all, as if she'd only imagined it. Except he did notice the tee-shirt.

She said she'd only grabbed it because it was there, because she hadn't wanted to disturb him, and he'd said, 'Yeah, right,' teasing her, looking pleased with himself. And then they had moved on, talking about Franc and the part, and he'd picked her up, spinning her round, full of thanks, and hope, and trepidation. Unfounded, because he'd smashed it.

But the tee-shirt was still here, shifting like an undertow. She could see glimpses of it surfacing now and again in his eyes, flashes of pleasure and curiosity, and it was giving her goose bumps. Tingles. Or maybe it wasn't in his eyes at all. Maybe it was just being with him that was making her tingle because that was all it seemed to take now: his presence. The scuff of his loafer, the swing of his arm, the curls clustering at his nape.

Oh, God! How was this happening? Swirling and swooning over her best friend, in so deep she couldn't tell left from right any more, couldn't tell what was or wasn't in his eyes. And maybe she ought to just come out with it, tell him she was in love with him, take the risk, get it over with for better or for worse.

Her heart clopped. Except, worse would be unbearable. Watching his face stiffen, the light in his eyes clouding, retreating, everything shrinking into a stunned, awkward silence.

No.

No, no, no.

She couldn't risk it, not without a definitive sign. More than a foot nudge. More than a momentary glimmer that could be read a million ways.

She drew in a breath, steadying herself. Better to wait, bide her time, enjoy the morning, the hour, the second, the moment… The brightening sky, the gentle warmth of the sun, the salt tang of the sea battling it out with the sweet smell of bread baking and Alden, standing on the quay, scanning the yachts in the marina, smiling round, twinkling.

'Which one would you have if you could pick one?'

She slid her eyes over the water. Sleek fancy

ones. Smaller, compact ones. Sparkling, glinting. But nothing was standing out.

'I don't think I can make a decision like that in a caffeine-depleted state.'

He grinned. 'You make a fair point.' And then he was turning, surveying the eateries on the opposite side. 'Bistrot Madeleine looks sweet. They've got flower thingies by the tables.' His eyes came to hers, flashing blue. 'Right up your street.'

She felt her breath catching, the love inside rising like a warm tide. Looking after her, wanting wherever they went to be *up her street*, because he was doing all this for her, wasn't he? Saint Tropez. Breakfast. Everything. But doing it as, what, a friend? Or because…?

Don't.

She flicked a glance at the bistro. Pale-green awning. Pale wicker chairs. And, by every table, a wicker planter overflowing with bright alstroemeria. Absolutely, one hundred percent, up her street.

She felt a smile coming. 'It's perfect.'

'Great!' He smiled and then his hand was catching hers, tugging her towards the café. 'Come on, let's go remedy the caffeine situation.'

He lifted his cup, sipping, trying to think of something to say, some conversation, but he had nothing. Just a scrabbling noise in his head, and a

knot tightening in his stomach. It was like being
sixteen again, stranded on that bed, holding his
breath. Walking was fine, and driving, because
motion in itself was a distraction. And last night
in bed, in the dark, he'd had the audition to talk
about, had needed to talk about it because he'd
been so happy, so damn high!

But with all that stripped away, what was left
was the tee-shirt, circling, hovering, consuming
him. The way she'd looked so utterly rumbled
when he'd teased her about it. For sure, she'd
bounced back quickly, supplying reasons. It had
been there, easy to pick up. She was trying to be
quiet so as not wake him, snatching it up instead
of rattling the wardrobe doors to get something
of her own. Credible reasons, yet he couldn't
quite…

It wasn't only the tee-shirt, though. It was the
light in her eyes too, the way it seemed to change
when she was looking at him. And every time
it happened he could feel his pulse quickening,
beating harder, desire stirring. All the old feelings rising, but stronger than before, spinning
him so fast he couldn't see straight or think
straight. All he could think was that he wanted
her to have put the tee-shirt on because it was
his, because she had feelings for him…

But he couldn't bring it up again any more than
he could ask her if she liked him that way, because what if her answer didn't match his hopes,

if the light in her eyes turned out to be just a figment of his own fertile imagination? Nothing would ever be the same between them.

Then again, after this week, were things ever going to be the same anyway? Faking an engagement, sharing a room, a bed; hugging, touching, growing closer… Things were already different. Their whole shape was changing. Maybe that was why he was teetering, quivering at the edge, thirty years old, feeling sixteen. He just needed a sign, a pointer, one way or the other. Then he'd know where he stood, know whether to stick or play. But how to draw a sign out of her when he couldn't even think of a single thing to say?

And then suddenly, blessedly, she was saving him the trouble.

'You're very quiet.' She frowned a little. 'Are you thinking about the part?'

As a good a subject as any, something he *could* talk about at least.

He set his cup down. 'I'm trying not to but, you know, it keeps creeping in…'

Like the tee-shirt.

'That's understandable. It's a big deal…' Her fingers went to her cup, twisting it back and forth. 'Such a pity we don't know who else is in the running… I don't suppose Joe Rubens would know?'

He felt affection surging. Always rooting for him, applying herself to his problems. If only she knew that, right now, *she* was the problem, the conundrum…

He shrugged. 'It's irrelevant. Knowing the competition isn't going to change anything. It's all down to Franc: who he feels is going to fit best. And the execs: who they're happy to back.' He felt a tingle. 'Ironically, I've got Natasha in my favour.'

'Natasha?' Jules's finger seemed to momentarily catch in her cup handle, slopping coffee. 'What do you mean?'

He felt his senses sitting up. Jules didn't have much love for Natasha, but there was something surfacing in her gaze right now that went beyond the usual protective animosity, something burning that looked more like…

His heart pulsed. But, without seeing more, without drawing more out of her, he couldn't be certain. Another pulse. He wasn't for poking bears, but he wanted, *needed*, to be certain…

He drew in a careful breath, fastening his eyes on hers, trying not to hate himself. 'What I mean is they know that Tash and I have great on-screen chemistry, that we look good together in love scenes.'

'But there aren't any love scenes in *Darkness*!' Jules's features seemed to be crowding into the middle of her face. 'Maeve and Saul's marriage falls apart; it's the story of a family breaking down. Mother, father, husband, wife—'

'You're right, but that's the book…' He paused to let the words sink in, then pushed home. 'The screenplay is different. Franc's written in a love scene because he wants to flash back to it from Saul's and Maeve's points of view, to show how things used to be between them before they hit the rocks.'

'Oh.' Her gaze fell. 'I didn't realise that was…' And then she was swallowing, looking up again, blinking. 'And how do you feel about it?'

Clearly better than she did.

He made his voice gentle. 'I feel okay.'

Her gaze flared. 'Really? You're okay with *kissing* her? Okay with…' she waved her hand '…all the rest?'

His heart clenched. She didn't *want* him kissing Natasha. It was all over her face, in her eyes. Feelings swirling… *Oh, God!* And hurt, filtering in, hurt that was the flipside of caring for someone, hurt that *he* was causing and had to stop *right now* because hurting her had never been the end game.

He planted his arms on the table, leaning towards her. 'I said I'm okay with it, not *relishing* it!'

Her eyes flickered, registering the words, the noise inside them quietening a little.

He felt relief rippling and, simultaneously, a chasm opening up. He might have got his answer, seen what he wanted to see, but it didn't mean he could wade in with some sweeping declaration, not after forcing her hand like that, bruising her in the process.

No. This wasn't the moment to be reaching for her hand, stroking his thumb over her skin, even if the urge was tugging at him hard. This was the moment to be righting the wheel, restoring the flow, which meant bringing her smile back.

He slid one eyebrow up, effecting a weary, the-atrical sigh. 'It's called *suffering* for one's art.'

She ran a tongue over her lip. 'Suffering?'

'Of *course*, suffering.' He rolled his eyes at her to help make the point. 'It's Natasha Forbes we're talking about!'

Throwing Tash under the bus wasn't exactly noble but he couldn't make himself care. It was Jules he cared about. *Loved!* With every smitten fibre of his being. From the moment she'd walked into Geography that day, the shy new girl with the warmest smile he'd ever seen. She'd caught his eye, beamed that smile right at him and that had been that.

All these years, pushing it down, hiding it, but there was no hiding it now. He could feel it ris-ing, glowing, lighting up his veins, his heart, and surely she was seeing it, because she was looking at him intently, taking him apart with her eyes, piece by helpless piece.

And then, suddenly her features were changing, softening, and her eyes were filling with a warm, lovely light. 'Natasha's not so bad.'

The unexpected words felt like release, like permission to land.

He let a chuckle loosen then shot her two fast glances, pantomime-style. 'Who are you, and what have you done with my best friend?'

She laughed, then leaned in with a conspiratorial glint. 'That's for me to know and you to wonder.' And then she was lifting her cup, looking at him over the rim, her eyes shining. 'Jokes aside, if you do get the part, then Natasha could turn out to be the gift that keeps on giving.'

More unexpected words.

'How so?'

She sipped and set her cup back down. 'Because it's *her*. Because you've got a past together, took a load of flak from the press. By working with her again as her leading man, smashing it out of the park, it'll actually give you more kudos than if it had been some other actress.'

'If it ever comes to pass, and we smash it out of the park, then it would give *both* of us kudos.'

One eyebrow cocked. 'True, but see, I don't really care about her one way or the other…' And then her gaze was softening, reaching in, turning off the breath to his lungs. 'I do care about you, though. Very much.'

CHAPTER SEVENTEEN

SHE EASED THE rudbeckia stem up a little, twisting it to make more of the flower head, then slotted it back into the vase.

'It's beautiful, Jules!'

Two hours working together and *finally* the housekeeper was calling her by her name instead of calling her *'mademoiselle'*.

'Thanks, Marie.' She looked up, catching the woman's smile with her own, then stepped away from the table, running her eyes over the low vases and mismatched glassware she'd set out along its length. She'd filled the vases with yesterday's lavender and rudbeckia, packing in freshly gathered rosemary, popped tea lights into the glasses, then woven a looping mass of young ivy vines through the lot to give it wildness, context, connection to the climbing jasmine and scrambling bougainvillea all around them.

She folded her arms. It *did* look good. Lavish. Theatrical. A little unkempt. She felt a tingle. *Oh, God!* It was like *her*, like a floral echo of what was going on inside her: twisting chaos, tingling happiness, tangling hope. She was restless, reckless weather. Thunder and lightning. A tugging breeze. Warm rain and sunshine. All at the same time, all because of Alden, because he liked her. *More* than liked her.

She felt a smile straining at her cheeks, a fizzy rush inside. All those glints and hints she'd been seeing in his eyes for days, glimmers that could have meant something or nothing, had come together in Saint Tropez, resolved into one long, deep, warm unequivocal look, a look that had stripped away every last shred of her doubt.

Unbelievable how it had even come about... talking about the Saul part, then Alden had brought up Natasha, and the love scene, and suddenly she'd been floundering, thinking: *How didn't I know?* Feeling sick to the stomach about it, trying not to show it but failing. *Clearly* failing.

Then he'd said something about Natasha, and about *suffering* for his art, and after that there had been a long still moment, something in his gaze shifting, like clouds parting, and suddenly she'd been looking at light, seeing the light, perhaps, drowning in his shades and colours, feeling her own shades and colours being drawn up and out. And then she knew what she was seeing; felt the knowledge arriving with a soft, liberating beat.

Liberating but silent. Nothing to grab or push off from. So she'd talked on about Natasha, listening to herself being upbeat and objective, amazed that she could even be like that. And then he'd delivered a cue and she'd seized it, told him she cared about him, loading her voice, her gaze, so he'd know what she was really saying.

And it had registered in his eyes, stirring warmth and movement. He'd opened his mouth to speak, but then the waitress had arrived with their breakfast and the moment had dissolved.

The moment but not the tingling knowledge. That had stayed, was with them, running, laughing, back to the car before their ticket ran out; with them in the car back to Cannes, singing along with those old songs. And it was in his eyes as he'd back-stepped away from her along the hall to that final script session.

It felt like a secret they were keeping, saving for later, saving for the right moment.

'Do you need anything else, Jules?'

Marie's voice broke in, pulling her back.

'No but thank you.' She went over to squeeze the woman's hand. 'I couldn't have done all this without you.'

Marie's features stretched in protest and then she was smiling, shrugging. 'It was fun, but now I must…how you say…? *Save* the dinner…' She rolled her eyes. 'Franc is running behind, so everything is—' Her hands went up, flapping, and then she was disappearing back through the French doors into the house.

Running behind?

Her heart sank. No chance of seeing Alden alone before dinner, then. No point lighting the candles or turning on the fairy lights that Marie had helped her weave through the jasmine.

She turned back to the table. On the other hand, running late meant she had time to go freshen up which, since she probably had ivy bugs in her hair, wouldn't be a bad thing. And what was waiting a bit longer after all this time anyway?

She leaned in to adjust the angle of a vase. No. Waiting was fine. She didn't mind waiting, not now that Alden had shown her the light in his eyes, not now that she could feel the change coming, tingling inside her. And at least she'd been able to put all the thrumming energy to work, styling the table, making the tiny keepsake bouquets for everyone to take away.

She stepped back. *Strange!* She wasn't worried any more about how the gesture might be interpreted, or that she wouldn't live up to Alden's hype. She was feeling stronger suddenly, sassier. She felt a smile coming. It was a good feeling.

CHAPTER EIGHTEEN

HE BROKE STRIDE, felt his breath standing down. Marie was right. Jules had created a miracle on the terrace. A midsummer night's dreamscape. Lights twinkling in the climbers, a multitude of candles flickering in a riot of green along the length of the table and, hanging off the ears of every chair, small bouquets tied with ivy.

So clever. So imaginative. But where was she?

And then suddenly her voice spun him round, stopping his heart. 'What do you think?'

She was coming towards him from the far end of the terrace, bare-shouldered and smiling, skirt flowing around her ankles. 'I thought I might as well use the stuff I got yesterday...'

Her eyes were glowing, full of candlelight, and something else that was making his pulse beat harder, his mouth run dry.

He swallowed. 'It's amazing!'

Pitiful!

Miles short, but it was all he could manage. *Crazy!* Because he was a talker, a non-stop driveller, but for some reason he couldn't quite launch. *Failure to Launch.* That was a movie, wasn't it? Starring...

Stop! Why was he thinking about that when there were things to say, when he'd expressly rushed out of that room ahead of everyone else so he could say them? But now all he could feel was panic rising. Maybe because the others were coming, their voices getting nearer, or maybe it was the cat getting his tongue again, the way it had after that waitress had stolen his moment in Saint Tropez. He hadn't been able to get that moment back. Not running to beat the ticket machine, not on the return drive, not even when her eyes had been holding him, all warm, as he'd walked backwards into that final script session.

And now she was looking at him like that again and he was stranded. Airwaves jammed. Transmission blocked.

How could he be thirty, trailing a playboy reputation everywhere he went, yet with Jules, still be tied into this knot of his sixteen-year-old self? Pounding inside. Scared. How was it that the hurdle of friendship seemed so much higher this close to, so much harder to scale? He didn't go in for heights, falling. The jarring crunch, the white flash of pain. Easier to buckle in, sit tight, except that all the evidence pointed to...

Oh, God! All afternoon, living for, with, on, that tingling knowledge, hanging on those words that had only skimmed the surface of what her eyes had been saying.

I care for you, very much.

And all he'd wanted, *all* he'd wanted, was to walk out here and say it back to her, kiss her like he should have kissed her in Saint Tropez, but now Trudi's voice was swooping in, other voices coming behind, which meant he was officially sunk.

'Oh, my… Did you do this, Jules?'

Jules shot him a quick smile and then she was sidestepping him. 'Yes, I did.'

'It's absolutely exquisite, my dear.' He could picture Trudi's chin tucked in; her eyes all lit up. 'Really, *really* lovely.'

'Thank you.'

Pleasure in Jules's voice, a smile. He could feel it infecting him, chasing the rest away. Maybe the others *were* intruding, stealing his moment, but he'd find a new moment, maybe a better one. For now, he couldn't not turn himself round and stand by her, watch her enjoying the praise she deserved.

'Goodness. Isn't this gorgeous!' Natasha was coming through the doors now, her eyes wide as saucers. 'It's *very* Lewis Carroll!'

'Lewis Carroll wasn't a florist, Natasha.' Trudi was being droll as only she could be, a girlish glint in her old-lady eyes.

'You're an old bat, Trudi Finch!' Natasha was laughing. 'You know very well what I meant. It's got a touch of the Mad Hatter about it.' Her eyes came to his briefly, and then her gaze slid to Jules. 'Bravo, Jules. I can see why Alden was waxing lyrical. You're quite the talent.'

He felt his heart pause. Would Jules throw off the compliment as she always did? He licked his lips, priming himself to dive in, but she wasn't stepping back, winding her fingers together. She was standing tall, smiling, emanating serenity.

'Thank you. You're very kind.' She gestured to the table. 'I had time on my hands, and the terrace lends itself to it, so I thought, why not have some fun? It's our last night, after all...'

He felt an up swell, warmth and pride surging. She was nailing it, shining, showing the light he'd always been able to see for miles. But then suddenly the voices around him were fading, and his chest was tightening, trying to close.

Last night...

It didn't automatically mean *last chance*, but still... Tomorrow was coming, closing in like walls. Taking the cute car back. Boarding the plane. Midday flight. Then it would be dropping her off first because she was in Richmond, saying goodbye in the taxi with the meter going and the driver watching, then home to pack for Cairo, leaving again the next day.

And she would be back in her shop, weaving her magic, or out dressing some venue, and if he didn't say something, *do* something, then who knew, maybe her thinking would start running in reverse. She might start noticing some other guy, *meet* some other guy who seemed…

And he wouldn't be there to stop her, to keep her eyes on his track—and then, abracadabra, he could find himself back in the friend zone. Cemented. *Condemned!* And maybe it wasn't crediting Jules with much, maybe it was just his stupid insecurity babbling, but he couldn't stop the thoughts coming, couldn't stop the panic beating.

He swallowed hard. He had to seize this night somehow, find a way to push through. He reached down, catching her hand, felt her fingers squeezing back. Did squeezing back mean she would come if he pulled her away right now, into the garden? Just a few moments to tell her, kiss her, pour love into—

'Jules…' Franc was coming towards them with outstretched arms, beaming. 'You've turned my humble terrace into a work of art. I stand here amazed.'

She split a grin. 'Excellent result!' And then she was laughing, putting her free hand on Franc's arm. 'I wanted to say thank you for having me here and saying it with flowers is what I do.'

'Well, you do it extremely well.'

Franc talked on, heaping on praise, making Jules blush a little, making her lips curve into that wide, sweet smile of hers.

Jules…

All those years, feeling knocked back by what her mum did, trying to hold her dad together, worrying about him; feeling as if she was losing him too. Then not getting the grades she should have got, in spite of *his* help, because she was distracted, toiling to settle.

Years trailing that wreckage—a little bit bruised, a little bit devalued because of it, but pushing herself on, finding a new creative direction. Tentative. Unsure. But working so hard. Leasing the shop. Worrying about it. Digging in, finding her feet, but always with that chink of fear at the edge of her gaze that it could all be ripped away. She'd been through the mill, paid her dues and now here she was, surrounded by a sea of admiring faces, faces belonging to people of influence.

He drew in a breath. No. He couldn't remove her, take *this* away from her. She needed it. Deserved it. He couldn't put himself in the way. He would wait…

'So, I'm curious, Jules…' Franc was cutting off a wedge of brie, transferring it to his plate. 'How did you and Alden meet?'

She felt a flutter starting, then receding again. They'd got their back story. School. Because it was true, because they could both talk about it easily. No snares. And Alden was right here beside her. Solid. Sheltering.

She looked at him quickly, checking in, then shot Franc a smile. 'Believe it or not, we were in the same class at school.'

'What?' Natasha's head swivelled. 'You were at school together?'

'That's right.' Alden set his glass down, signalling with his eyes that he was saving her from the inquisition. 'Halcyon days, eh? Riding the school bus, bunking off social studies.'

Movie afternoons, curtains drawn, his fresh-air smell, the tantalising touch of his foot, the tingling agony of nothing happening...

Trudi picked up the baton. 'So were you high-school sweethearts, then?'

Her heart paused.

The truth.

No snares.

'No.' She shook her head. 'We weren't together at school—'

'But you must have *liked* each other, surely?'

Her heart stopped.

No snares. Except for the one she'd just stepped into, the one that was busy sending a heatwave ebbing up her spine, stripping the breath from her lungs.

And she couldn't look at Alden for help because they hadn't talked about this, had they, hadn't talked about anything. It was all so nebulous still, shimmering in the ether, that tingling knowledge, tingling even now, pulsing between them. But nothing had been said. Aired. *Released!*

It had seemed as if he wanted to talk earlier, bursting onto the terrace, a bit breathless, a bit tense, but then everyone had arrived, and the moment had gone. And now Trudi's eyes were burning into hers, flitting to him—back, forth, back, and forth—and all she could feel was the silence stretching, inexplicable to everyone else at the table, her tongue sliding around for words, and then suddenly it was Alden's voice breaking the silence, making her heart bounce.

'*I* did.' Little pause. 'I liked Jules…'

And then before she could catch her breath, he was turning, fastening hesitant, hopeful eyes on hers. 'I liked you from the moment you walked into Geography.'

Her first day at Fullerton! He'd liked her from day one. *Day one!*

A soft plea surfaced in his gaze. 'Remember…?'

Her heart gave. How could she ever forget? Walking in. That descending hush. Heads turning, eyes staring, the teacher saying her name. Belly pulsing. Shoes pinching. A scratchy label somewhere. And then, his face. Blue eyes beaming light and kindness in her direction, making the rest disappear.

Same as now.

Same as *right now.*

She swallowed. 'Of course I remember. I was terrified, feeling sick.'

'I could see that but, even so, you smiled at me and that was…' His lips parted slightly, stiffening. 'Enough to…' And then, as if he'd just remembered the others, he turned back to the table. 'You must understand that I was the nerdiest kid in the class, so a smile from such as Jules was a smiting blow to my poor dorky heart.'

Making light. Making himself the butt of a joke that wasn't a joke at all. She felt tears prickling, scalding her lids. Saying it to them but speaking to *her*. Love at first sight. Love he'd kept hidden.

Oh, God! Too many things to count all making sense now. Never asking her anything about her boyfriends but always mopping her up after they left, being the dependable shoulder, the one saying she was too good for them, making her smile again. Always there for her.

Her heart pulsed. If only he'd said something. Nudged twice! Why the hell hadn't he nudged twice?

And now—*now*—he was busy pinning his heart to his sleeve in front of all these people who couldn't possibly understand what was going on, and she *couldn't* sit silent—*couldn't*—not when her heart was right here, bursting, ready to be pinned right next to his.

'You weren't a nerd, Alden. Ever!'

His gaze swung back, registering her tears,

softening, and intensifying in the same beat. Such a look. Scrambling her insides, shredding her composure but she couldn't make herself care. Not now. If this was to be their stage, then so be it.

She put her hands to his face to shut out the others. 'You were a total sweetheart. Still are. Brainy, yes, but you were never a swot, or a suck-up, or a know-it-all. Not a social incompetent. Not uncool. Ever!'

Could he see the love inside her, feel it flowing? She stroked her thumbs over his cheekbones, fighting the crack that was threatening her voice. 'You were literally the best thing in that school. And out of it, for that matter.'

A swell moved behind his gaze. 'Jules...'

He was getting it now, understanding at last. She felt warmth pulsing, running through her veins, a sudden boldness arriving. She moved in, pressing her forehead to his, lowering her voice to a whisper. 'You are, and always have been, the best thing.'

For a beat he seemed to stop breathing, and then his forehead rolled against hers. 'No, Jules, not me. That's you...' And then suddenly his hands were coming to her face, making their bubble tighter. 'Have you any idea how much I want to kiss you right now?'

She felt her limbs unstringing, a low ache tugging. His voice was unrecognisable. Lower than a whisper. Urgent. Hot like wire. The voice of a lover, not a friend.

She pressed her head into his, keeping her voice lower than low. 'Yes, because I want to kiss you too—'

'I can't be doing with all this *tête à tête* business!' Trudi's voice arrowed in, mock chiding. 'You clearly adored each other at school. So why no romance? And how did you finally get together?'

Alden's jaw contracted beneath her hands. 'We need an escape plan.'

Something quick. Incontestable. Her mind wheeled, and then she had it. She pressed in closer, whispering to his cheek. 'You start talking. I'll throw you a cue.'

His cheek lifted, smiling, making her want to smile too. 'Never missed one yet.' And then he was disengaging, turning back to the table. 'Apologies.' He flashed his electric smile. 'We were having a little moment there.' And then his hand went up, raking at his hair. 'Trudi, to answer your question, I think that maybe—'

'Oh, my God, Alden!'

His head whipped round, eyes signalling approval at the high drama.

'You've got to call Barclay, remember?' She pointed to her watch, tapping it for good measure. 'Ten o'clock, wasn't it? It's two minutes to!'

She held her breath. What would he do with

it? A random name. A time imperative. It ought to be enough. He'd always been good at improvisation.

And then his hands were going down onto the table. 'Ah!'

It was a nice, long exhale threaded through with exactly the right amount of regret. She exhaled herself, carefully, trying not to smile.

'Sorry, folks...' He pushed up from his chair, reaching to pull her up too, shrugging helplessness. 'Barclay's the second unit director for my shoot next week. I got a shouty-capitals message earlier to call him at ten.' More shrugging. 'I can only assume it's important.'

He nodded goodnight to Franc, then smiled at Trudi. 'Sorry, Tee. We'll have to do *part deux* another time.'

Were any of them convinced? Franc's smile was as enigmatic as ever, and she couldn't bring herself to bump gazes with Natasha or to look properly at Trudi. All she could manage was a general smile and a goodnight, and then Alden was tugging her away, across the terrace and through the doors.

CHAPTER NINETEEN

HE FLUNG HIS hand backwards, groping for the switch. 'Light on or off?'

Her fingers stilled in his hair momentarily. 'Leave it off.' And then her lips were on his neck again, scorching his skin. 'I like moonlight.' One breathless hand slid down to his crotch, launching a fire bolt through his veins. 'It's romantic, don't you think?'

'Yeah.' He gritted his teeth to stop a groan exploding from his throat. Her hand was stroking him through his chinos, making his erection pulse and harden more. He could feel his eyes rolling backwards under his lids, his limbs unstringing. She was undoing his button now, feeling for his zip, but going down that road would only end in tears.

With an effort he came back to the moment, taking her face in his hands to kiss her again, distract her.

Lips. Face. More lips. So soft. Warm. *Perfect.* Moulding to his, kissing him back; yielding, letting him in; tangling, stroking, drawing heat through him like zip wire.

He broke off to catch his breath, but instantly she was pulling him back, kissing him deeply, making little catching sounds in her throat, clawing at his shirt buttons, pushing hot hands under, and then her hands were sliding down again, to his rear now, exploring, kneading, stroking.

He felt a throb in his belly, or maybe it was a sob, because this wasn't a fantasy of Jules. It *was* Jules. *Her* lips, *her* hands, *her* body, right here, pressing into him, wanting him.

Him...

But no more than he wanted her. He was hard, pulsing, somewhat out of his body, or was that a slave to hers?

He ran his hands down the sides of her neck to her shoulders. Smooth. *Delectable.* He bent his head. *Kissable.* And then his hands bumped into soft cotton: flounces, rowing him back to the terrace. Bare-shouldered Jules, coming towards him...

'This *top* is romantic.' He pushed at the fabric and suddenly her hands were there too, helping, yanking it down.

She let out a breathless little chuckle. 'It's called a Bardot top so, you know, appropriate.' And then she was unhooking her bra, drawing his hands to her breasts.

He felt a fresh groan lodging low down in his

throat, desire exploding in his veins. Soft, full, filling his hands perfectly. Nipples hardening for his thumbs, thumbs making her gasp. He wanted to look, to see her properly, but they seemed to be some distance from the light switch now, and besides, she liked the moonlight. He *had* to taste her, though.

He scooped her up, felt her legs winding tightly around him as he carried her to the bed. And then they were crashing together, fighting the duvet; then her breasts were there again, warm, soft, and smooth. He found a nipple, drawing it into his mouth. She moaned and a current arced, forking through him. He couldn't get enough of her. He sucked, then used his thumb, circling and teasing, then his mouth again, until she was arching her back, beating her fists on the bed. 'Please, Alden, please…'

His pulse spiked. He knew what she wanted, didn't need asking again. He raised himself up to move, but then her face turned, catching a spill of moonlight, and he forgot how.

Flushed cheeks. Milky skin. Crazy hair.

Everything he'd ever wanted, right here.

He felt his heart cracking, a dry whisper emerging. 'Jules…'

She blinked, the haze in her eyes clearing, and then her hand came up, flattening against his cheek. 'I love you, Alden.'

His heart cracked wide and then a hard pulse

of desire thundered, blazing through his veins. He leaned in, taking her mouth with his, loading his kiss with all the love he was feeling inside. He could feel her fingers moving in his hair, sliding to his nape, caressing—every touch, heaven… and hell. Bringing him to life…killing him. Because this was Jules—*Jules*—making his throat ache, making him want to sob, making his blood pump and his erection pulse, bringing him closer, closer…

He broke away, fighting for breath, then he moved himself backwards, pushing her skirt up, stroking his hands along her thighs, going slowly to heighten her anticipation, and to gather himself back in. And then he lowered himself, trembling, to his knees.

Was he really doing this, with *her*—sliding his hands all the way up, hooking his fingers into her underwear to draw it down her legs? Long legs—sublime. Legs that deserved some attention. He felt his throat catching, a tremor running through him as he pressed his lips to the inside of her thigh. Her skin was smooth and so, so soft. He let his tongue loose, slowly running it higher, until suddenly her body tensed.

'No!' She sat up, pulling at his arms. 'Not that way…' Her voice was thick, barely recognisable. She pressed a hand to her chest. 'I want to feel you here. Your heart next to mine.'

And then she was pulling him down and her hands were unzipping him, freeing him.

His pulse lunged. He could feel his blood coursing, roaring in his ears, feel patches of her skin scorching. He heard a strangled sound rumbling its way up his throat, heard himself asking if it was safe, if she was—

'Yes… It's okay…' Her mouth came to his: hot, breathless, and tender.

And that was all he needed. He didn't care that they still had bits of their clothes on, or that he was going in unarmed. All he wanted was to please her, love her, unravel inside her.

'Jules…' His lips were grazing hers, making her blood tingle, setting off that ache again low down in her belly. She closed her eyes. Never in her life had anyone loved her the way he just had, made her feel so loved. Three times—every time more exquisite than the last—and now he was kissing her again, nuzzling her neck. 'Are you happy?'

She felt her heart filling, a smile curving. 'What do *you* think?' She doodled a slow circle on his back. 'I'm like a cat drowning in cream.'

He laughed. 'Good.' And then he lay down, pulling her into his arms.

She snuggled in, breathing in his smell, feeling her body loosening, her heart flying free.

If Trudi hadn't asked that question, would they have pushed through by themselves, got to this sublime place? Or would they still have been on opposite sides of the bed, friends instead of lovers?

She stroked her fingers over the smooth warmth of his chest, liking the firm swell of his muscles, the little valley in between. Maybe he wouldn't want to talk right now, but she wanted to know, couldn't not ask. She pressed her lips to his skin. 'Why did you never say anything?'

His body tensed for a fraction of a second, and then his hand slipped over hers.

'Because I was scared.' His chest lifted on a breath. 'No matter what you said downstairs, fact is, when you started at Fullerton, I *was* a nerd. I'd never had a girlfriend, didn't know how to kiss. Absolutely no one had ever fancied me.'

Her heart gave. 'But you were adorable.'

'Puppies are adorable. I wanted to be one of the cool boys, and I wasn't. So when you smiled at me…' His arm tightened around her, conveying the rest. And then his lips were moving in her hair.

'It meant even more when you turned out to be beautiful on the inside as well as the outside. You listened to me—*really* listened to me—when I was talking about movies and acting. You didn't try to change the subject or hurry me along, and it was such a release, because I couldn't talk about that stuff at home, couldn't dream about it with anyone. And I knew I couldn't replace that, couldn't risk wrecking it by coming onto you...

'And then your mum left and *you* were the one who needed someone to talk to—to rant and rail at—and I wanted it to be me, wanted to be a friend to you the way you were to me. And you let me. And we got close but, the closer we got, the harder it got for me to say anything. You were so crushed by what your mum did. You kept saying you couldn't understand how she could be two different people—one thing at home but all the time carrying on behind your backs...'

His voice tightened. 'I didn't want you to think I was like that, Jules: that I wasn't the friend you thought I was. I didn't want you to think that I had an agenda.'

She felt her eyes welling, an ache spreading. As if she could ever have thought such a thing. 'Oh, Alden...'

His hand moved, caressing hers. 'Then you started going out with other boys, and they weren't anything like me, so I figured that I'd never have stood a chance anyway.'

She felt a frown coming. 'What do you mean, they weren't like you?'

'They were tall, usually dark-haired, sporty...'

Like Hayden! Clearly, he was still carrying that particular remnant around in his box of insecurities.

She turned her hand over, lacing her fingers

into his. 'FYI, they were also the ones who *asked* me! I'd have taken you over them any day.'

He let out a short, amused breath. 'How was I to know that?'

She felt a smile coming. 'You'd have known if you'd nudged twice.'

'What?'

She shifted, propping herself up on one elbow so she could see his face in the half-light. 'You used to nudge my foot sometimes when we were watching your movies, didn't you?'

His eyebrows went up. 'You knew?'

'No! I *wondered*. And that's the whole point! Your strategy was flawed. One nudge isn't enough. It could be accidental. Unintentional. Two nudges, three, four, basically any number greater than one is saying something. Two nudges and I might have nudged back.'

'Okay.' His eyebrows drew in, concentrating. 'Two nudges. Got it!' And then his foot tapped hers: once, twice...

She felt a giggle vibrating and leaned in to kiss him. And then he was responding, rising to meet her, kissing her back. She felt heat stirring, happiness bursting. 'I'm just so glad we're here, Alden, finally, thanks to Trudi.'

'So am I...' His tongue was teasing hers now, triggering hot little darts.

She felt a smile coming. 'What on earth must they all have thought?'

His hands came to her face. 'We don't care, Jules, okay?' His eyes were dark, full of wicked glow, full of promise. 'Now—' his lips brushed hers '—I nudged you twice, so please be a good little fiancée and let me ravish you.'

CHAPTER TWENTY

The present...

HE TURNED AWAY from the door, clamping his hands
to his head, fighting the burn that was scorching
up his throat, scalding his lids.

What have I done?

Why the hell had he let the panic in, listened
to it, let it control him? It had all been so perfect,
better than perfect. A dream coming true: Jules.
His at last. Kissing her, loving her. Out of body
with it, out of his mind, and she'd been loving
him back, filling him up, filling his senses, stealing his breath.

No! Not stealing. She didn't have to. Everything he'd given, he'd given freely, from the heart.
Breath. Body. Soul. All the love. One hundred
percent. Opened out. Laid bare. Nothing else left.

Except to fall.

Oh, and how he'd fallen. Spectacularly. Ruin-
ously. Doing the worst possible thing he could do

to her. And that was why she wasn't opening the door, he got it, but he *had* to make her. Somehow.

He sucked in a breath and spun, using his fists. 'Jules, please…' He gulped down a sob, hammering. 'Please, Jules, I'm begging you, let me explain. Give me that at least.'

Silence.

Stretching.

And then a snib-click, the door giving under the weight of his hands.

No Jules on the other side.

He shuddered. Letting him cross the threshold alone. A slap in the face. Nothing less than he deserved. He picked up his holdall and went in.

She was standing by the sitting-room window, arms folded, defensive. *Of course*. Her face was silent, tight, and pale. Because of him. Shadows under her eyes because of him. His heart cracked. Eyes like marble because of him.

He mustered some breath. 'Thanks for opening…' His heart twisted. She wasn't giving him anything—not an inch, not even a blink.

Maybe if I was closer…

As if she was reading his mind, her body stiffened, stopping him in his tracks.

He felt a fresh scald stinging behind his lids, a tremor affecting his jaw. Letting him in but shutting him out. To hurt him back, to see him burn. He deserved it, yes, but how could he get any words out when he was hurting this hard?

He looked at his feet, trying to draw in air. But he must get the words out. He'd walked off set for this, ditched the film for this, ruined his reputation for this, so he had to man up now and say his piece, for what it was worth.

He forced himself to look up and meet her gaze. 'I'm sorry, Jules. I can't even begin to—' Her arms tightened across her front, twisting the knife. 'I don't expect you to forgive me. I'm not asking for that.'

Only hoping, because what else was left now but hope, hope that she would somehow understand?

He swallowed, sifting through the muddle inside. 'Natasha was right about me, Jules. I only gave her sixty percent—if that. It's all I've ever given anyone.' He could feel a band tightening inside his head, aching. 'The thing is, I didn't know it, had no idea, until we...'

He bit down hard on his lip. Would she scoff if he used those words? Would her eyebrows lift in derision? He swallowed again. 'You were always the dream, Jules. My unreachable star. And somehow, in Cannes, I finally got to touch you, hold you, love you. And it was...'

Tears were welling in her eyes now, glistening, ripping his heart at the seams, making his voice want to crack, but he had to keep going, let all of it out.

'It was the most sublime, moving, incredible

night of my life. Suddenly I knew, *knew*, what one hundred percent felt like. How it felt to give it, and to receive it…'

And she did too. It was in her eyes behind the tears and all the questions he had to answer somehow.

He inhaled to steady himself. 'When I woke up, you were sleeping.' *Sweet-faced, tumble-haired, angelic.* 'You looked so lovely.' Her lips pinched, tightening a cord in his throat. 'I was looking at you, in wonder, to be honest, amazed that you loved me, and then I started thinking about that hundred percent, started worrying that maybe my hundred percent wouldn't be good enough, and that if everything I had to give wasn't good enough for you then you would be disappointed and I'd see it in your eyes, and it would be unbearable.'

'So you thought you'd just up and leave?' Her tears were flowing now, sliding down her cheeks.

He felt his heart crashing, a sob coming. 'I wasn't *thinking*. I was *panicking*. Don't you understand? You're perfect, Jules. Always have been. Gold standard from head to toe: warm, compassionate, funny, gifted, beautiful. It's why I've never been able to make it with anyone else, I see that now.

'You blind me. I'm saturated to my bones with love for you, but that morning, I couldn't switch off the panic, the voice in my head saying, "what if?". What if I proved incapable of the kind of love you deserve? What if I broke your heart, hurt you the way your mum hurt you?'

He felt darkness cramming the edge of his vision, bitterness exploding inside. 'All I've ever done is disappoint the people who love me, Jules. And there I was, looking at you, all in for one hundred percent—an *untested* one hundred percent. And suddenly I was terrified of my feelings for you—how deep they went. Terrified that in the end they wouldn't be enough, that *I* wouldn't be enough. That I'd turn out to be another fricking disappointment; that we'd end up with less than we started with, and so, God help me, I…'

He pressed his fingers hard into his head. He was going round in circles, repeating himself, and clearly none of it was washing with her. He felt his heart wilting, withering. Why would it?

He let his hand fall. 'I know it doesn't make sense, knew it the moment I landed in Cairo. I should have called you then, but I was so bloody wretched. I didn't know how I'd ever be able to explain it, so I went to a bar, stayed…'

'And the next day you thought, what?' She was coming towards him suddenly, arms pegged tight, eyes blazing wet. 'I'll just ignore all these messages from my dream girl, from my unreachable star, let her stew in the pain I've caused her?'

He felt his ears growing hot, his heart crashing again. 'I lost my phone when I was—'

'Drunk?'

He nodded.

'And you couldn't have borrowed one?'

'Yes, but I don't know your number by heart.'
Oh, the irony. 'You're my number one on speed
dial.'

'Weak, Alden!' She was practically snarling now.
'I've got a shop! A website! You could have—'

His heart seized. 'I didn't know what to say
to you, all right!'

Her body stiffened and instantly he felt a flash
of heat and shame. It had come out too loud, too
ragged.

He inhaled, softening his voice. 'I thought
you'd hate me. Expected it! And I couldn't face
it, didn't want to see the pain I'd caused you.'

'But you're here now...' Her eyes were welling again, her mouth buckling. 'Too late, I might
add, in case you're wondering.'

His heart split. 'Don't say that. Please...' He
forced his gaze to hold hers, to not swerve. 'I'm
here because I love you, Jules. What I did is un-
forgivable, but I *do* love you—you must believe
me. I screwed up in the worst possible way, I
know that, but I came to my senses, *decided* it
was time for me to grow up, grow a pair, be the
kind of man you'd want me to be.

'I walked off the film, got a phone and a flight.
I looked up the shop, got your number, called to
say I was coming—not that I was expecting you

to answer. And now here I am. Sick with myself.
Facing the music.'

Something surfaced momentarily in her gaze
then vanished.

'Fine.' She swallowed, and then she was going
over to the bookcase, collecting something, coming back with it.

His throat closed. Grandmother's ring box.

She cracked the hinge, revealing the glitter inside, then she snapped it shut and held it out. 'Take
this with you. And, please, close the door on your
way out.'

CHAPTER TWENTY-ONE

Three weeks later...

SHE FELT HER stomach roiling as she passed through the gates. *Nerves!* And then, rolling in behind, another one of those queasy waves. As if she needed reminding.

Oh, God!

Would he be here? And would they *ever* catch a break?

Three weeks. Soul-searching. Aching. Hating him one second, missing him the next, not knowing what to feel...

Daring to come across her threshold like that, *daring* to say he loved her after doing the exact same thing Mum had done. It was all she could think about while he'd been sliding around in the mess he'd made; all she'd been able to think about for days afterwards. The betrayal. That *he* could have done that to her—*him*, of all people. Round and round in her head—the thing she couldn't forget. *Forgive.*

But then a small voice inside had started bending her ear, whispering that it wasn't the same as with Mum, because Mum hadn't come back to face the music. She hadn't stood in the pool of misery she'd caused, trying to explain herself. Mum hadn't cut work to come and see her, even though she'd been nowhere near as far away as Cairo. But Alden had.

The press had seized on it, of course.

She felt her sinuses tingling, tears prickling. He would have hated that, would have known it was coming. But still he'd walked off set and done it anyway, for *her*, so he could see her, explain. And yes, better not to have done the thing that needed explaining in the first place, but still it spoke to something, didn't it, that he would put himself through that for her, put her above everything else?

The small voice had gone on. Always there for her through the years, through thick and thin. Hiding his love because he hadn't wanted her to think he had an agenda, hiding it because he'd put her on some kind of stupid pedestal, so high that he didn't dare to reach up, reach out, nudge twice!

It was his pattern, what he did with those actors he admired too. Seeming to be so easy with them on the surface but always with that little shirt tail hanging, that stubborn insecurity that wouldn't let him go, that flung him time and time

again into that introspective maze. Overanalys-
ing. Overthinking. Getting himself lost and tangled. It was why he turned to her, talked to her,
listened to her advice.

But that morning in Cannes she'd been asleep
at the crucial moment, asleep while he was busy
losing faith in himself, panicking. And for once
he hadn't woken her up. For some stupid reason,
he'd bolted, bolted so hard and so fast that he
couldn't find a way back. Until he had.

He said he'd decided to grow up, be the kind
of man she wanted him to be. Her heart caught.
But that was the thing, wasn't it? He already was
the kind of man she wanted him to be. Yes, he
was insecure, but he was so many other things
as well. Funny, kind, warm. Generous to a fault.
And maybe part of her own needy soul loved that
he needed her too, loved that he was the yin to
her yang. She loved him still, in spite of everything. Couldn't imagine not loving him…

She let her gaze drift to the tall beeches flank-
ing the path, their leaves just starting to turn.
It all came down to love in the end. She could
either cut Alden off the way she had cut Mum
off—let the sun set on everything they'd ever
been and shared—or bend, focus on the good,
on all the love, accept that he had his failings,
as she had hers.

Oh, yes! No matter what he thought, she wasn't
perfect, not by a long chalk. She'd hung on too

tightly to the hurt Mum caused. Hung onto it for years—letting it close her off, letting it stop her from giving fully, trusting fully—and because of that she'd hurt plenty of people on her own account, like Sam.

She'd had to choose a path, make a decision, and when she did, she'd felt her heart lifting to the rooftops, all her colours coming back. She'd grabbed her diary, to see where Alden was this week—because she always wrote it down—but then her eyes had snagged on the 'month to view' box, the absence of the red dot she always used…

She'd scrabbled through the bathroom drawer. Found the packet.

Two missed pills.

How?

Two missed pills. One passionate night on the French Riviera.

She felt tears prickling again. She wasn't sad about the baby. How could she be when it was theirs, a little mix of the two of them? It was joyful. Overwhelming. But the timing was terrible. So much to put on him all at once. That she loved him, wanted to be with him, wanted them to try… *And, by the way, you're going to be a father.*

He stared across the Serpentine, trying not to let his hopes leap. Hard, though, because she'd called him. Called. Him. Three aching weeks of silence, dodging the paps, Jacklyn tearing him off a strip every five minutes—and then, this morning, finally, it had been *her* voice at the end of the line. Would he see her, meet her on their usual bridge?

As if wild horses could stop him!

Jules wanting to see him could only be a good sign, a sign that maybe they could be friends again. He'd take that, if it was all she could offer, because everything hurt without her, because life without Jules was—

'Alden…?'

Her voice spun him round, springing his heart clear of his body.

'Jules…'

Pale still, but her gaze was warm, wide, a little gleam just visible at its edges. He felt his heart settling, filling. She looked like herself again, not like the ceramic-eyed creature who'd given him back his ring, along with his marching orders, three weeks ago.

Her fingers chased a stray lock behind her ear. 'Thanks for coming.'

His heart seized a little. 'Did you think I wouldn't?'

'No but…' She seemed nervous. 'After the way we—' She frowned, correcting herself. 'The way *I* was, I—'

'Hey.' Was she really taking this on herself? *Not fair.* He closed the distance between them, only just managing not to take hold of her shoulders. 'I deserved everything you dished out, and more.'

'No.' She shook her head, and then her eyebrows were doing their adorable up-and-down dance. 'Well, yes, you did, but I don't want to dwell on it, not any more.' She let out a sigh, and then her gaze was softening into his, making his hope beat harder.

'I'm tired of thinking about it, Alden, tired of holding onto hurt.' Her lips pressed together. 'It's what I did with Mum—what I'm still doing—but I can't do it with you, I just can't, not when I know you, know that whatever particular brand of crazy was going on in your head that morning, you didn't *mean* to hurt me.'

His heart gave. Was she really saying these words that sounded like forgiveness? He felt his throat trying to close, a fierce heat prickling behind his lids. He didn't deserve her kindness. He wanted it, craved it, but he didn't deserve it.

'No, I didn't. But—'

Her finger came to his lips, stopping his flow. 'But nothing. You upset your director for me, flew back to see me. And when I weigh that up against you leaving me in Cannes, I can only think that the one probably balances out the other.'

Balances out...?

He searched her gaze, heart drumming. 'What are you saying?' Because right now he needed clarity. He could feel his body trembling, his bonds straining, hope, and love climbing his walls. But he couldn't risk a wrong foot now, assume he was in if he was out. He licked his lips. 'Are we friends again, or…?'

She caught her bottom lip between her teeth, and then there it was, that little sparkle coming back into her eyes, tears and light mingling. 'I'm very much thinking along the lines of *or*…as in, picking up from that night, going forward again from there…'

His heart stopped, and then it was exploding, showering joy. A do-over! A chance to put things right, to prove his love. Prove he could give more than a hundred percent and keep on giving it every day, hour, minute, second—for ever. He owed her that and so much more. *His* Jules. His heart. His one and only Jules.

'Oh, Jules…' He took her face into his hands. 'I don't deserve this, don't deserve you, but I promise you, I won't screw up again.'

She smiled into his eyes. 'I know that.'

He felt a fresh burn starting behind his lids. She believed in him! In spite of everything. Believed in him, as she always had. He felt his limbs loosening, peace and warmth blooming in his chest. He was safe now; finally he was in the only place he'd ever wanted to be.

He let his eyes loose in hers. 'I love you, Jules. So very, very much.'

'I love you too, Alden.'

Such a look in her eyes, a look to drown in.

He stroked her cheekbones, catching a flare of heat in her gaze, feeling it flaring inside himself. 'I can't wait to show you, *prove* it to you—starting from right now.' He leaned in, drawing on a line he'd used before, one that was sure to make her smile. 'Have you any idea how much I want to kiss you right now?'

'I've got a hunch…' Her eyes were wet, smiling, full of everything. 'But before we get to that, there's just one more thing…'

EPILOGUE

Eighteen months later...

'CONGRATULATIONS, ALDEN! Best Actor! How does it feel to be holding the statue?'

Best Actor in a Franc Abdali film! How to even answer?

Getting the nomination for Saul had been shocking enough, although not to Jules. She was convinced from the moment Franc showed her some of the dailies.

He'd been more circumspect. For sure, he'd put everything into it, laid himself out, but in doing that he'd only exposed himself to a truck load of anxiety about the quality of his performance.

Thank God for Jules, grounding him, keeping him level. Believing in him. A year on, he was coming round to the view that he'd made a decent fist of it, but he'd never expected a nomination, let alone to win the bloody thing.

He felt the smooth heft of the statue in his hands. How to encapsulate what it meant? His parents were here, full of smiles, and he was pleased to see them, pleased that they were proud of him at last.

But he'd stopped obsessing about their approval that day in Cannes when Jules had interceded for him with Franc. He'd kicked free that day, chosen to rise. And, aside from the stupid panic that had sent him fleeing to Cairo, he'd been comfortable with every single one of his life and career choices since then.

But the NKV News correspondent, Ted Blint, didn't want to hear about all that. Ted was after a pithy sound bite.

He smiled at Ted, going for brevity. 'It feels amazing.' He put a hand to his neck, tilting his head to avoid the glare of the flashguns.

'And what about that acceptance speech, huh?' Ted's eyebrows were arching all the way into his fake hairline. 'Your wife was looking pretty emotional out there, but not as emotional as you!'

He winced inside, then felt a smile creasing his cheeks. Satisfying to hear that Jules had been moved. He'd seen her eyes glistening at the start, a smile lifting her cheeks as she'd caught on that he was keeping his long-ago promise to thank her first.

But then suddenly he'd lost it, found himself tearing up, gulping out words, thanking her for being his lover, his wife, his best friend. Sobbing thanks to Franc, to the crew, to his co-stars, and probably to the dog too, eyes too full and wet to see her face any more, to see anything at all. And then he'd felt the host's hand on his arm, signalling that it was time for him to clear the stage, and he'd made to go the wrong way and had had to be rescued and redirected. Not exactly his finest hour, but still, she'd asked for 'over-egged'!

He met Ted's gaze. 'Well, it's an emotional moment, obviously, and my wife—' His heart caught. Suddenly he couldn't find the words, only feel the love inside coming in great big swells. He owed Jules everything. Owed her for this statue. For Honey, their beautiful daughter. For saving him. Every day.

He swallowed hard, felt tears regrouping behind his eyes. He couldn't do this, couldn't stand here talking to Ted when she was inside waiting for him. This was Hollywood fluff. This didn't matter, but she did.

He licked his top lip and smiled. 'Actually, I think my wife probably wants to kiss me right now, and I definitely want to kiss her so, if you don't mind, I'm going to say thank you and goodnight.'

* * * * *